Defoe Abbott Marx Hardy Machiavelli Chesterton Emerson Joyce Austen
Melville Montaigne Cooper Hugo Eliot Grimm
Stoker Carroll Christie Haggard Molière Schiller
Wilde Maupassant Byron Engels Smith Kafka Hall
Garnett Fitzgerald Hawthorne Dostoyevsky Willis
Goethe Einstein Kipling Doyle
Cotton Henry Nietzsche Balzac
Baum Leslie Dumas Flaubert Turgenev Crane
Stockton Vatsyayana Verne Vinci
Burroughs Gogol Busch
Curtis Tocqueville Whitman
Homer Widger Tolstoy
Darwin Thoreau Twain Scott Plato Harte
Potter Freud Zola Lawrence Dickens Hesse
Kant Jowett Stevenson Burton
Andersen Cervantes
London Descartes Voltaire
Poe Aristotle Wells Cooke
Hale James Hastings Irving
Bunner Shakespeare
Richter Chekhov Chambers da Shaw Benedict Alcott
Doré Dante Wodehouse Pushkin
Swift Newton

There's Pippins and Cheese to Come

Charles Stephen Brooks

Imprint

This book is part of TREDITION CLASSICS

Author: Charles Stephen Brooks
Cover design: Buchgut, Berlin – Germany

Publisher: tredition GmbH, Hamburg - Germany
ISBN: 978-3-8424-2387-9

www.tredition.com
www.tredition.de

THERE'S PIPPINS AND CHEESE TO COME

There's Pippins and Cheese To Come

In my noonday quest for food, if the day is fine, it is my habit to shun the nearer places of refreshment. I take the air and stretch myself. Like Eve's serpent I go upright for a bit. Yet if time presses, there may be had next door a not unsavory stowage. A drinking bar is nearest to the street where its polished brasses catch the eye. It holds a gilded mirror to such red-faced nature as consorts within. Yet you pass the bar and come upon a range of tables at the rear.

Now, if you yield to the habits of the place you order a rump of meat. Gravy lies about it like a moat around a castle, and if there is in you the zest for encounter, you attack it above these murky waters. "This castle hath a pleasant seat," you cry, and charge upon it with pike advanced. But if your appetite is one to peck and mince, the whiffs that breathe upon the place come unwelcome to your nostrils. In no wise are they like the sweet South upon your senses. There is even a suspicion in you — such is your distemper — that it is too much a witch's cauldron in the kitchen, "eye of newt, and toe of frog," and you spy and poke upon your food. Bus boys bear off the crockery as though they were apprenticed to a juggler and were only at the beginning of their art. Waiters bawl strange messages to the cook. It's a tongue unguessed by learning, yet sharp and potent. Also, there comes a riot from the kitchen, and steam issues from the door as though the devil himself were a partner and conducted here an upper branch. Like the man in the old comedy, your belly may still ring dinner, but the tinkle is faint. Such being your state, you choose a daintier place to eat.

Having now set upon a longer journey—the day being fine and the sidewalks thronged—you pass by a restaurant that is but a few doors up the street. A fellow in a white coat flops pancakes in the window. But even though the pancake does a double somersault and there are twenty curious noses pressed against the glass, still you keep your course uptown.

Nor are you led off because a near-by stairway beckons you to a Chinese restaurant up above. A golden dragon swings over the door. Its race has fallen since its fire-breathing grandsire guarded the fruits of the Hesperides. Are not "soys" and "chou meins" and other such treasures of the East laid out above? And yet the dragon dozes at its post like a sleepy dog. No flame leaps up its gullet. The swish of its tail is stilled. If it wag at all, it's but in friendship or because a gust of wind has stirred it from its dreams.

I have wondered why Chinese restaurants are generally on the second story. A casual inquiry attests it. I know of one, it is true, on the ground level, yet here I suspect a special economy. The place had formerly been a German restaurant, with Teuton scrolls, "Ich Dien," and heraldries on its walls. A frugal brush changed the decoration. From the heart of a Prussian blazonry, there flares on you in Chinese yellow a recommendation to try "Our Chicken Chop Soy." The quartering of the House of Hohenzollern wears a baldric in praise of "Subgum Noodle Warmein," which it seems they cook to an unusual delicacy. Even a wall painting of Rip Van Winkle bowling at tenpins in the mountains is now set off with a pigtail. But the chairs were Dutch and remain as such. Generally, however, Chinese restaurants are on the second story. Probably there is a ritual from the ancient days of Ming Ti that Chinamen when they eat shall sit as near as possible to the sacred moon.

But hold a bit! In your haste up town to find a place to eat, you are missing some of the finer sights upon the way. In these windows that you pass, the merchants have set their choicest wares. If there is any commodity of softer gloss than common, or one shinier to the eye—so that your poverty frets you—it is displayed here. In the window of the haberdasher, shirts—mere torsos with not a leg below or head above—yet disport themselves in gay neckwear. Despite their dismemberment they are tricked to the latest turn of fashion. Can vanity survive such general amputation? Then there is hope for immortality.

But by what sad chance have these blithe fellows been disjointed? If a gloomy mood prevails in you—as might come from a bad turn of the market—you fancy that the evil daughter of Herodias still lives around the corner, and that she has set out her victims to the general view. If there comes a hurdy-gurdy on the street and you cock your ear to the tune of it, you may still hear the dancing measure of her wicked feet. Or it is possible that these are the kindred of Holofernes and that they have supped guiltily in their tents with a sisterhood of Judiths.

Or we may conceive—our thoughts running now to food—that these gamesome creatures of the haberdasher had dressed themselves for a more recent banquet. Their black-tailed coats and glossy shirts attest a rare occasion. It was in holiday mood, when they were fresh-combed and perked in their best, that they were cut off from life. It would appear that Jack Ketch the headsman got them when they were rubbed and shining for the feast. We'll not squint upon his writ. It is enough that they were apprehended for some rascality. When he came thumping on his dreadful summons, here they were already set, fopped from shoes to head in the newest whim. Spoon in hand and bib across their knees—lest they fleck their careful fronts—they waited for the anchovy to come. And on a sudden they were cut off from life, unfit, unseasoned for the passage. Like the elder Hamlet's brother, they were engaged upon an act that had no relish of salvation in it. You may remember the lamentable child somewhere in Dickens, who because of an abrupt and distressing accident, had a sandwich in its hand but no mouth to put it in. Or perhaps you recall the cook of the Nancy Bell and his grievous end. The poor fellow was stewed in his own stew-pot. It was the Elderly Naval Man, you recall—the two of them being the ship's sole survivors on the deserted island, and both of them lean with hunger—it was the Elderly Naval Man (the villain of the piece) who "ups with his heels, and smothers his squeals in the scum of the boiling broth."

And yet by looking on these torsos of the haberdasher, one is not brought to thoughts of sad mortality. Their joy is so exultant. And all the things that they hold dear—canes, gloves, silk hats, and the newer garments on which fashion makes its twaddle—are within reach of their armless sleeves. Had they fingers they would be smoothing themselves before the glass. Their unbodied heads, wherever they may be, are still smiling on the world, despite their divorcement. Their tongues are still ready with a jest, their lips still parted for the anchovy to come.

A few days since, as I was thinking—for so I am pleased to call my muddy stirrings—what manner of essay I might write and how best to sort and lay out the rummage, it happened pat to my needs that I received from a friend a book entitled "The Closet of Sir Kenelm Digby Knight Opened." Now, before it came I had got so far as to select a title. Indeed, I had written the title on seven different sheets of paper, each time in the hope that by the run of the words I might leap upon some further thought. Seven times I failed and in the end the sheets went into the waste basket, possibly to the confusion of Annie our cook, who may have mistaken them for a reiterated admonishment towards the governance of her kitchen—at the least, a hint of my desires and appetite for cheese and pippins.

"The Closet of Sir Kenelm Digby Opened" is a cook book. It is due you to know this at once, otherwise your thoughts—if your nature be vagrant—would drift towards family skeletons. Or maybe the domestic traits prevail and you would think of dress-clothes hanging in camphorated bags and a row of winter boots upon a shelf.

I am disqualified to pass upon the merits of a cook book, for the reason that I have little discrimination in food. It is not that I am totally indifferent to what lies on the platter. Indeed, I have more than a tribal aversion to pork in general, while, on the other hand, I quicken joyfully when noodles are interspersed with bacon. I have a tooth for sweets, too, although I hold it unmanly and deny it as I can. I am told also—although I resent it—that my eye lights up on the appearance of a tray of French pastry. I admit gladly, however, my love of onions, whether they come hissing from the skillet, or lie in their first tender whiteness. They are at their best when they are placed on bread and are eaten largely at midnight after society has done its worst.

A fine dinner is lost within me. A quail is but an inferior chicken—a poor relation outside the exclusive hennery. Terrapin sits low

in my regard, even though it has wallowed in the most aristocratic
marsh. Through such dinners I hack and saw my way without even
gaining a memory of my progress. If asked the courses, I balk after
the recital of the soup. Indeed, I am so forgetful of food, even when
I dine at home, that I can well believe that Adam when he was ques-
tioned about the apple was in real confusion. He had or he had not.
It was mixed with the pomegranate or the quince that Eve had
sliced and cooked on the day before.

A dinner at its best is brought to a single focus. There is one dish
to dominate the cloth, a single bulk to which all other dishes are
subordinate. If there be turkey, it should mount from a central platter. Its protruding legs out-top the candles. All other foods are, as it
were, privates in Caesar's army. They do no more than flank the
pageant. Nor may the pantry hold too many secrets. Within reason,
everything should be set out at once, or at least a gossip of its coming should run before. Otherwise, if the stew is savory, how shall
one reserve a corner for the custard? One must partition himself
justly — else, by an over-stowage at the end, he list and sink.

I am partial to picnics — the spreading of the cloth in the woods or
beside a stream — although I am not avid for sandwiches unless
hunger press me. Rather, let there be a skillet in the company and
let a fire be started! Nor need a picnic consume the day. In summer
it requires but the late afternoon, with such borrowing of the night
as is necessary for the journey home. You leave the street car, clank-
ing with your bundles like an itinerant tinman. You follow a stream,
which on these lower stretches, it is sad to say, is already infected
with the vices of the city. Like many a countryman who has come to
town, it has fallen to dissipation. It shows the marks of the bottle.
Further up, its course is cleaner. You cross it in the mud. Was it not
Christian who fell into the bog because of the burden on his back?
Then you climb a villainously long hill and pop out upon an open
platform above the city.

The height commands a prospect to the west. Below is the smoke
of a thousand suppers. Up from the city there comes the hum of life,
now somewhat fallen with the traffic of the day — as though Nature
already practiced the tune for sending her creatures off to sleep.
You light a fire. The baskets disgorge their secrets. Ants and other

leviathans think evidently that a circus has come or that bears are in the town. The chops and bacon achieve their appointed destiny. You throw the last bone across your shoulder. It slips and rattles to the river. The sun sets. Night like an ancient dame puts on her jewels:

> And now that I have climbed and won this height,
> I must tread downward through the sloping shade
> And travel the bewildered tracks till night.
> Yet for this hour I still may here be stayed
> And see the gold air and the silver fade
> And the last bird fly into the last light.

By these confessions you will see how unfit I am to comment on the old cook book of Sir Kenelm Digby. Yet it lies before me. It may have escaped your memory in the din of other things, that in the time when Oliver Cromwell still walked the earth, there lived in England a man by the name of Kenelm Digby, who was renowned in astrology and alchemy, piracy, wit, philosophy and fashion. It appears that wherever learning wagged its bulbous head, Sir Kenelm was of the company. It appears, also, that wherever the mahogany did most groan, wherever the possets were spiced most delicately to the nose, there too did Sir Kenelm bib and tuck himself. With profundity, as though he sucked wisdom from its lowest depth, he spouted forth on the transmutation of the baser metals or tossed you a phrase from Paracelsus. Or with long instructive finger he dissertated on the celestial universe. One would have thought that he had stood by on the making of it and that his judgment had prevailed in the larger problems. Yet he did not neglect his trencher.

And now as time went on, the richness of the food did somewhat dominate his person. The girth of his wisdom grew no less, but his body fattened. In a word, the good gentleman's palate came to vie with his intellect. Less often was he engaged upon some dark saying of Isidore of Seville. Rather, even if his favorite topic astrology were uppermost about the table, his eye travelled to the pantry on every change of dishes. His fingers, too, came to curl most delicately on his fork. He used it like an epicure, poking his viands apart for sharpest scrutiny. His nod upon a compote was much esteemed.

Now mark his further decline! On an occasion—surely the old rascal's head is turned!—he would be found in private talk with his hostess, the Lady of Middlesex, or with the Countess of Monmouth, not as you might expect, on the properties of fire or on the mortal diseases of man, but—on subjects quite removed. Society, we may be sure, began to whisper of these snug parleys in the arbor after dinner, these shadowed mumblings on the balcony when the moon was up—and Lady Digby stiffened into watchfulness. It was when they took leave that she saw the Countess slip a note into her lord's fingers. Her jealousy broke out. "Viper!" She spat the words and seized her husband's wrist. Of course the note was read. It proved, however, that Sir Kenelm was innocent of all mischief. To the disappointment of the gossips, who were tuned to a spicier anticipation, the note was no more than a recipe of the manner that the Countess was used to mix her syllabub, with instruction that it was the "rosemary a little bruised and the limon-peal that did quicken the taste." Advice, also, followed in the postscript on the making of tea, with counsel that "the boiling water should remain upon it just so long as one might say a *miserere*." A mutual innocence being now established, the Lady Digby did by way of apology peck the Countess on the cheek.

Sir Kenelm died in 1665, full of years. In that day his fame rested chiefly on his books in physic and chirurgery. His most enduring work was still to be published—"The Closet Opened."

It was two years after his death that his son came upon a bundle of his father's papers that had hitherto been overlooked. I fancy that he went spying in the attic on a rainy day. In the darkest corner, behind the rocking horse—if such devices were known in those distant days—he came upon a trunk of his father's papers. "Od's fish," said Sir Kenelm's son, "here's a box of manuscripts. It is like that they pertain to alchemy or chirurgery." He pulled out a bundle and held it to the light—such light as came through the cobwebs of the ancient windows. "Here be strange matters," he exclaimed. Then he read aloud: "My Lord of Bristol's Scotch collops are thus made: Take a leg of fine sweet mutton, that to make it tender, is kept as long as possible may be without stinking. In winter seven or eight days"—"Ho! Ho!" cried Sir Kenelm's son. "This is not alchemy!" He drew out another parchment and read again: "My Lord of Carlile's sack posset, how it's made: Take a pottle of cream and boil in it a little whole cinnamon and three or four flakes of mace. Boil it until it simpreth and bubbleth."

By this time, as you may well imagine, Sir Kenelm's son was wrought to an excitement. It is likely that he inherited his father's palate and that the juices of his appetite were stirred. Seizing an armful of the papers, he leaped down the attic steps, three at a time. His lady mother thrust a curled and papered head from her door and asked whether the chimney were afire, but he did not heed her. The cook was waddling in her pattens. He cried to her to throw wood upon the fire.

That night the Digby household was served a delicacy, red herrings broiled in the fashion of my Lord d'Aubigny, "short and crisp and laid upon a sallet." Also, there was a wheaten flommery as it was made in the West Country — for the cook chose quite at random — and a slip-coat cheese as Master Phillips proportioned it. Also, against the colic, which was ravishing the country, the cook prepared a metheglin as Lady Stuart mixed it — "nettles, fennel and grumel seeds, of each two ounces being small-cut and mixed with honey and boiled together." It is on record that the Lady Digby smiled for the first time since her lord had died, and when the grinning cook bore in the platter, she beat upon the table with her spoon.

The following morning, Sir Kenelm's son posted to London bearing the recipes, with a pistol in the pocket of his great coat against the crossing of Hounslow Heath. He went to a printer at the Star in Little Britain whose name was H. Brome.

Shortly the book appeared. It was the son who wrote the preface: "There needs no Rhetoricating Floscules to set it off. The Authour, as is well known, having been a Person of Eminency for his Learning, and of Exquisite Curiosity in his Researches. Even that Incomparable Sir Kenelme Digbie Knight, Fellow of the Royal Society and Chancellour to the Queen Mother, (Et omen in Nomine) His name does sufficiently Auspicate the Work." The sale of the book is not recorded. It is supposed that the Lady Middlesex, so many of whose recipes had been used, directed that her chair be carried to the shop where the book was for sale and that she bought largely of it. The

Countess of Dorset bought a copy and spelled it out word for word to her cook. As for the Lady Monmouth, she bought not a single copy, which neglect on coming to the Digbys aroused a coolness.

To this day it is likely that a last auspicated volume still sits on its shelf with the spice jars in some English country kitchen and that a worn and toothless cook still thumbs its leaves. If the guests about the table be of an antique mind, still will they pledge one another with its honeyed drinks, still will they pipe and whistle of its virtues, still will they —

"EAT" — A flaring sign hangs above the sidewalk. By this time, in our noonday search for food, we have come into the thick of the restaurants. In the jungle of the city, here is the feeding place. Here come the growling bipeds for such bones and messes as are thrown them.

The waiter thrusts a card beneath my nose. "Nice leg of lamb, sir?" I waved him off. "Hold a bit!" I cried. "You'll fetch me a capon in white broth as my Lady Monmouth broileth hers. Put plentiful sack in it and boil it until it simpreth!" The waiter scratched his head. "The chicken pie is good," he said. "It's our Wednesday dish." "Varlet!" I cried — then softened. "Let it be the chicken pie! But if the cook knoweth the manner that Lord Carlile does mix and pepper it, let that manner be followed to the smallest fraction of a pinch!"

On Buying Old Books

By some slim chance, reader, you may be the kind of person who, on a visit to a strange city, makes for a bookshop. Of course your slight temporal business may detain you in the earlier hours of the day. You sit with committees and stroke your profound chin, or you spend your talent in the market, or run to and fro and wag your tongue in persuasion. Or, if you be on a holiday, you strain yourself on the sights of the city, against being caught in an omission. The bolder features of a cathedral must be grasped to satisfy a quizzing neighbor lest he shame you later on your hearth, a building must be stuffed inside your memory, or your pilgrim feet must wear the pavement of an ancient shrine. However, these duties being done and the afternoon having not yet declined, do you not seek a bookshop to regale yourself?

Doubtless, we have met. As you have scrunched against the shelf not to block the passage, but with your head thrown back to see the titles up above, you have noticed at the corner of your eye — unless it was one of your blinder moments when you were fixed wholly on the shelf — a man in a slightly faded overcoat of mixed black and white, a man just past the nimbleness of youth, whose head is plucked of its full commodity of hair. It was myself. I admit the portrait, though modesty has curbed me short of justice.

Doubtless, we have met. It was your umbrella — which you held villainously beneath your arm — that took me in the ribs when you lighted on a set of Fuller's Worthies. You recall my sour looks, but it was because I had myself lingered on the volumes but cooled at the price. How you smoothed and fingered them! With what triumph you bore them off! I bid you — for I see you in a slippered state, eased and unbuttoned after dinner — I bid you turn the pages with a slow thumb, not to miss the slightest tang of their humor. You will of course go first, because of its broad fame, to the page on Shakespeare and Ben Jonson and their wet-combats at the Mermaid. But before the night is too far gone and while yet you can hold yourself from nodding, you will please read about Captain John Smith of Virginia and his "strange performances, the scene whereof is laid at such a distance, they are cheaper credited than confuted."

In no proper sense am I a buyer of old books. I admit a bookish quirk maybe, a love of the shelf, a weakness for morocco, especially if it is stained with age. I will, indeed, shirk a wedding for a bookshop. I'll go in "just to look about a bit, to see what the fellow has," and on an occasion I pick up a volume. But I am innocent of first editions. It is a stiff courtesy, as becomes a democrat, that I bestow on this form of primogeniture. Of course, I have nosed my way with pleasure along aristocratic shelves and flipped out volumes here and there to ask their price, but for the greater part, it is the plainer shops that engage me. If a rack of books is offered cheap before the door, with a fixed price upon a card, I come at a trot. And if a brown dust lies on them, I bow and sniff upon the rack, as though the past like an ancient fop in peruke and buckle were giving me the courtesy of its snuff box. If I take the dust in my nostrils and chance to sneeze, it is the fit and intended observance toward the manners of a former century.

I have in mind such a bookshop in Bath, England. It presents to the street no more than a decent front, but opens up behind like a swollen bottle. There are twenty rooms at least, piled together with such confusion of black passages and winding steps, that one might think that the owner himself must hold a thread when he visits the remoter rooms. Indeed, such are the obscurities and dim turnings of the place, that, were the legend of the Minotaur but English, you might fancy that the creature still lived in this labyrinth, to nip you between his toothless gums—for the beast grows old—at some darker corner. There is a story of the place, that once a raw clerk having been sent to rummage in the basement, his candle tipped off the shelf. He was left in so complete darkness that his fears overcame his judgment and for two hours he roamed and babbled among the barrels. Nor was his absence discovered until the end of the day when, as was the custom, the clerks counted noses at the door. When they found him, he bolted up the steps, nor did he cease his whimper until he had reached the comforting twilight of the outer world. He served thereafter in the shop a full two years and had a beard coming—so the story runs—before he would again venture beyond the third turning of the passage; to the stunting of his scholarship, for the deeper books lay in the farther windings.

Or it may appear credible that in ages past a jealous builder contrived the place. Having no learning himself and being at odds with those of better opportunity, he twisted the pattern of the house. Such was his evil temper, that he set the steps at a dangerous hazard in the dark, in order that scholars—whose eyes are bleared at best—might risk their legs to the end of time. Those of strict orthodoxy have even suspected the builder to have been an atheist, for they have observed what double joints and steps and turnings confuse the passage to the devouter books—the Early Fathers in particular being up a winding stair where even the soberest reader might break his neck. Be these things as they may, leather bindings in sets of "grenadier uniformity" ornament the upper and lighter rooms. Biography straggles down a hallway, with a candle needed at the farther end. A room of dingy plays—Wycherley, Congreve and their crew—looks out through an area grating. It was through even so foul an eye, that when alive, they looked upon the world. As for theology, except for the before-mentioned Fathers, it sits in general and dusty convention on the landing to the basement, its snuffy sermons, by a sad misplacement—or is there an ironical intention?—pointing the way to the eternal abyss below.

It was in this shop that I inquired whether there was published a book on piracy in Cornwall. Now, I had lately come from Tintagel on the Cornish coast, and as I had climbed upon the rocks and looked down upon the sea, I had wondered to myself whether, if the knowledge were put out before me, I could compose a story of Spanish treasure and pirates. For I am a prey to such giddy ambition. A foul street—if the buildings slant and topple—will set me thinking delightfully of murders. A wharf-end with water lapping underneath and bits of rope about will set me itching for a deep-sea plot. Or if I go on broader range and see in my fancy a broken castle on a hill, I'll clear its moat and sound trumpets on its walls. If there is pepper in my mood, I'll storm its dungeon. Or in a softer moment I'll trim its unsubstantial towers with pageantry and rest upon my elbow until I fall asleep. So being cast upon the rugged Cornish coast whose cliffs are so swept with winter winds that the villages sit for comfort in the hollows, it was to be expected that my thoughts would run toward pirates.

There is one rock especially which I had climbed in the rain and fog of early morning. A reckless path goes across its face with a sharp pitch to the ocean. It was so slippery and the wind so tugged and pulled to throw me off, that although I endangered my dignity, I played the quadruped on the narrower parts. But once on top in the open blast of the storm and safe upon the level, I thumped with desire for a plot. In each inlet from the ocean I saw a pirate lugger— such is the pleasing word—with a keg of rum set up. Each cranny led to a cavern with doubloons piled inside. The very tempest in my ears was compounded out of ships at sea and wreck and pillage. I needed but a plot, a thread of action to string my villains on. If this were once contrived, I would spice my text with sailors' oaths and such boasting talk as might lie in my invention. Could I but come upon a plot, I might yet proclaim myself an author.

With this guilty secret in me I blushed as I asked the question. It seemed sure that the shopkeeper must guess my purpose. I felt myself suspected as though I were a rascal buying pistols to commit a murder. Indeed, I seem to remember having read that even hardened criminals have become confused before a shopkeeper and betrayed themselves. Of course, Dick Turpin and Jerry Abershaw could call for pistols in the same easy tone they ordered ale, but it would take a practiced villainy. But I in my innocence wanted nothing but the meager outline of a pirate's life, which I might fatten to my uses.

But on a less occasion, when there is no plot thumping in me, I still feel a kind of embarrassment when I ask for a book out of the general demand. I feel so like an odd stick. This embarrassment applies not to the request for other commodities. I will order a collar that is quite outside the fashion, in a high-pitched voice so that the whole shop can hear. I could bargain for a purple waistcoat—did my taste run so—and though the sidewalk listened, it would not draw a blush. I have traded even for women's garments—though this did strain me—without an outward twitch. Finally, to top my valor, I have bought sheet music of the lighter kind and have pronounced the softest titles so that all could hear. But if I desire the poems of Lovelace or the plays of Marlowe, I sidle close up to the shopkeeper to get his very ear. If the book is visible, I point my thumb at it without a word.

It was but the other day—in order to fill a gap in a paper I was writing—I desired to know the name of an author who is obscure although his work has been translated into nearly all languages. I wanted to know a little about the life of the man who wrote *Mary Had a Little Lamb*, which, I am told, is known by children over pretty much all the western world. It needed only a trip to the Public Library. Any attendant would direct me to the proper shelf. Yet once in the building, my courage oozed. My question, though serious, seemed too ridiculous to be asked. I would sizzle as I met the attendant's eye. Of a consequence, I fumbled on my own devices, possibly to the increase of my general knowledge, but without gaining what I sought.

They had no book in the Bath shop on piracy in Cornwall. I was offered instead a work in two volumes on the notorious highwaymen of history, and for a moment my plot swerved in that direction. But I put it by. To pay the fellow for his pains—for he had dug in barrels to his shoulders and had a smudge across his nose—I bought a copy of Thomson's "Castle of Indolence," and in my more energetic moods I read it. And so I came away.

On leaving the shop, lest I should be nipped in a neglect, I visited the Roman baths. Then I took the waters in the Assembly Room. It was Sam Weller, you may recall, who remarked, when he was entertained by the select footmen, that the waters tasted like warm flat-irons. Finally, I viewed the Crescent around which the shirted Winkle ran with the valorous Dowler breathing on his neck. With such distractions, as you may well imagine, Cornish pirates became as naught. Such mental vibration as I had was now gone toward a tale of fashion in the days when Queen Anne was still alive. Of a consequence, I again sought the bookshop and stifling my timidity, I demanded such volumes as might set me most agreeably to my task.

I have in mind also a bookshop of small pretension in a town in Wales. For purely secular delight, maybe, it was too largely composed of Methodist sermons. Hell fire burned upon its shelves with a warmth to singe so poor a worm as I. Yet its signboard popped its welcome when I had walked ten miles of sunny road. Possibly it was the chair rather than the divinity that keeps the place in memory. The owner was absent on an errand, and his daughter, who had been clumping about the kitchen on my arrival, was uninstructed in the price marks. So I read and fanned myself until his return.

Perhaps my sluggishness toward first editions—to which I have hinted above—comes in part from the acquaintance with a man who in a linguistic outburst as I met him, pronounced himself to be a numismatist and philatelist. One only of these names would have satisfied a man of less conceit. It is as though the pteranodon should claim also to be the spoon-bill dinosaur. It is against modesty that one man should summon all the letters. No, the numismatist's head is not crammed with the mysteries of life and death, nor is a philatelist one who is possessed with the dimmer secrets of eternity. Rather, this man who was so swelled with titles, eked a living by selling coins and stamps, and he was on his way to Europe to replenish his wares. Inside his waistcoat, just above his liver—if he owned so human an appendage—he carried a magnifying glass. With this, when the business fit was on him, he counted the lines and dots upon a stamp, the perforations on its edge. He catalogued its volutes, its stipples, the frisks and curlings of its pattern. He had numbered the very hairs on the head of George Washington, for in such minutiae did the value of the stamp reside. Did a single hair spring up above the count, it would invalidate the issue. Such values, got by circumstance or accident—resting on a flaw—founded on a speck—cause no ferment of my desires.

For the buying of books, it is the cheaper shops where I most often prowl. There is in London a district around Charing Cross Road where almost every shop has books for sale. There is a continuous rack along the sidewalk, each title beckoning for your attention. You recall the class of street-readers of whom Charles Lamb wrote—"poor gentry, who, not having wherewithal to buy or hire a book, filch a little learning at the open stalls." It was on some such street that these folk practiced their innocent larceny. If one shopkeeper frowned at the diligence with which they read "Clarissa," they would continue her distressing adventures across the way. By a lingering progress up the street, "Sir Charles Grandison" might be nibbled down—by such as had the stomach—without the outlay of a single penny. As for Gibbon and the bulbous historians, though a whole perusal would outlast the summer and stretch to the colder months, yet with patience they could be got through. However, before the end was come even a hasty reader whose eye was nimble on the page would be blowing on his nails and pulling his tails between him and the November wind.

But the habit of reading at the open stalls was not only with the poor. You will remember that Mr. Brownlow was addicted. Really, had not the Artful Dodger stolen his pocket handkerchief as he was thus engaged upon his book, the whole history of Oliver Twist must have been quite different. And Pepys himself, Samuel Pepys, F.R.S., was guilty. "To Paul's Church Yard," he writes, "and there looked upon the second part of Hudibras, which I buy not, but borrow to read." Such parsimony is the curse of authors. To thumb a volume cheaply around a neighborhood is what keeps them in their garrets. It is a less offence to steal peanuts from a stand. Also, it is recorded in the life of Beau Nash that the persons of fashion of his time, to pass a tedious morning "did divert themselves with reading in the booksellers' shops." We may conceive Mr. Fanciful Fopling in the sleepy blink of those early hours before the pleasures of the day have made a start, inquiring between his yawns what latest novels have come down from London, or whether a new part of "Pamela" is offered yet. If the post be in, he will prop himself against the shelf and—unless he glaze and nod—he will read cheaply for an hour. Or my Lady Betty, having taken the waters in the pump-room and lent her ear to such gossip as is abroad so early, is now handed to her chair and goes round by Gregory's to read a bit. She is flounced to the width of the passage. Indeed, until the fashion shall abate, those more solid authors that are set up in the rear of the shop, must remain during her visits in general neglect. Though she hold herself against the shelf and tilt her hoops, it would not be possible to pass. She is absorbed in a book of the softer sort, and she flips its pages against her lap-dog's nose.

But now behold the student coming up the street! He is clad in shining black. He is thin of shank as becomes a scholar. He sags with knowledge. He hungers after wisdom. He comes opposite the bookshop. It is but coquetry that his eyes seek the window of the tobacconist. His heart, you may be sure, looks through the buttons at his back. At last he turns. He pauses on the curb. Now desire has clutched him. He jiggles his trousered shillings. He treads the gutter. He squints upon the rack. He lights upon a treasure. He plucks it forth. He is unresolved whether to buy it or to spend the extra shilling on his dinner. Now all you cooks together, to save your business, rattle your pans to rouse him! If within these ancient buildings there are onions ready peeled—quick!—throw them in the skillet that the whiff may come beneath his nose! Chance trembles and casts its vote—eenie meenie—down goes the shilling—he has bought the book. Tonight he will spread it beneath his candle. Feet may beat a snare of pleasure on the pavement, glad cries may pipe across the darkness, a fiddle may scratch its invitation—all the rumbling notes of midnight traffic will tap in vain their summons upon his window.

Any Stick Will Do To Beat A Dog

Reader, possibly on one of your country walks you have come upon a man with his back against a hedge, tormented by a fiend in the likeness of a dog. You yourself, of course, are not a coward. You possess that cornerstone of virtue, a love for animals. If at your heels a dog sniffs and growls, you humor his mistake, you flick him off and proceed with unbroken serenity. It is scarcely an interlude to your speculation on the market. Or if you work upon a sonnet and are in the vein, your thoughts, despite the beast, run unbroken to a rhyme. But pity this other whose heart is less stoutly wrapped! He has gone forth on a holiday to take the country air, to thrust himself into the freer wind, to poke with his stick for such signs of Spring as may be hiding in the winter's leaves. Having been grinding in an office he flings himself on the great round world. He has come out to smell the earth. Or maybe he seeks a hilltop for a view of the fields that lie below patched in many colors, as though nature had been sewing at her garments and had mended the cloth from her bag of scraps.

On such a journey this fellow is travelling when, at a turn of the road, he hears the sound of barking. As yet there is no dog in sight. He pauses. He listens. How shall one know whether the sound comes up a wrathful gullet or whether the dog bays at him impersonally, as at the distant moon? Or maybe he vents himself upon a stubborn cow. Surely it is not an idle tune he practices. He holds a victim in his mind. There is sour venom on his churlish tooth. Is it best to go roundabout, or forward with such a nice compound of innocence, boldness and modesty as shall satisfy the beast? If one engross oneself on something that lies to the lee of danger, it allays suspicion. Or if one absorb oneself upon the flora—a primrose on the river's brim—it shows him clear and stainless. The stupidest dog should see that so close a student can have no evil in him. Perhaps it would be better to throw away one's stick lest it make a show of violence. Or it may be concealed along the outer leg. Ministers of Grace defend us, what an excitement in the barnyard! Has virtue no reward? Shall innocence perish off the earth? Not one dog, but many, come running out. There has gone a rumor about the barn that there is a stranger to be eaten, and it's likely—if they keep their clamor—there will be a bone for each. Note how the valor oozes from the man of peace! Observe his sidling gait, his skirts pulled close, his hollowed back, his head bent across his shoulder, his startled eye! Watch him mince his steps, lest a lingering heel be nipped! Listen to him try the foremost dog with names, to gull him to a belief that they have met before in happier circumstances! He appeals mutely to the farmhouse that a recall be sounded. The windows are tightly curtained. The heavens are comfortless.

You remember the fellow in the play who would have loved war had they not digged villainous saltpetre from the harmless earth. The countryside, too, in my opinion, would be more peaceful of a summer afternoon were it not overrun with dogs. Let me be plain! I myself like dogs—sleepy dogs blinking in the firelight, friendly dogs with wagging tails, young dogs in their first puppyhood with their teeth scarce sprouted, whose jaws have not yet burgeoned into danger, and old dogs, too, who sun themselves and give forth hollow, toothless, reassuring sounds. When a dog assumes the cozy habits of the cat without laying off his nobler nature, he is my friend. A dog of vegetarian aspect pleases me. Let him bear a mild eye as though he were nourished on the softer foods! I would wish every dog to have a full complement of tail. It's the sure barometer of his warm regard. There's no art to find his mind's construction in the face. And I would have him with not too much curiosity. It's a quality that brings him too often to the gate. It makes him prone to sniff when one sits upon a visit. Nor do I like dogs addicted to sudden excitement. Lethargy becomes them better. Let them be without the Gallic graces! In general, I like a dog to whom I have been properly introduced, with an exchange of credentials. While the dog is by, let his master take my hand and address me in softest tones, to cement the understanding! At bench-shows I love the beasts, although I keep to the middle of the aisle. The streets are all the safer when so many of the creatures are kept within.

Frankly, I would enjoy the country more, if I knew that all the dogs were away on visits. Of course, the highroad is quite safe. Its frequent traffic is its insurance. Then, too, the barns are at such a distance, it is only a monstrous anger can bring the dog. But if you are in need of direction you select a friendly white house with green shutters. You swing open the gate and crunch across the pebbles to the door. To the nearer eye there is a look of "dog" about the place. Or maybe you are hot and thirsty, and there is a well at the side of the house. Is it better to gird yourself to danger or to put off your thirst until the crossroads where pop is sold?

Or a lane leads down to the river. Even at this distance you hear the shallow brawl of water on the stones. A path goes off across a hill, with trees beckoning at the top. There is a wind above and a wider sweep of clouds. Surely, from the crest of the hill the whole county will lie before you. Such tunes as come up from the world below—a school-bell, a rooster crowing, children laughing on the road, a threshing machine on the lower meadows—such tunes are pitched to a marvellous softness. Shall we follow the hot pavement, or shall we dare those lonely stretches?

There is a kind of person who is steeped too much in valor. He will cross a field although there is a dog inside the fence. Goodness knows that I would rather keep to the highroad with such humility as shall not rouse the creature. Or he will shout and whistle tunes that stir the dogs for miles. He slashes his stick against the weeds as though in challenge. One might think that he went about on unfeeling stalks instead of legs as children walk on stilts, or that a former accident had clipped him off above the knees and that he was now jointed out of wood to a point beyond the biting limit. Or perhaps the clothes he wears beneath—the inner mesh and very balbriggan of his attire—is of so hard a texture that it turns a tooth. Be these defenses as they may, note with what bravado he mounts the wall! One leg dangles as though it were baited and were angling for a bite.

There is a French village near Quebec whose population is chiefly dogs. It lies along the river in a single street, not many miles from the point where Wolfe climbed to the Plains of Abraham. There are a hundred houses flat against the roadway and on the steps of each there sits a dog. As I went through on foot, each of these dogs picked me up, examined me nasally and passed me on, not generously as though I had stood the test, but rather in deep suspicion that I was a queer fellow, not to be penetrated at first, but one who would surely be found out and gobbled before coming to the end of the street. As long as I would eventually furnish forth the common banquet, it mattered not which dog took the first nip. Inasmuch as I would at last be garnished for the general tooth, it would be better to wait until all were gathered around the platter. "Good neighbor dog," each seemed to say, "you too sniff upon the rogue! If he be honest, my old nose is much at fault." Meantime I padded lightly through the village, at first calling on the dogs by English names, but later using such wisps as I had of French. "Aucassin, mon pauvre chien. Voici, Tintagiles, alors donc mon cherie. Je suis votre ami," but with little effect.

But the dogs that one meets in the Canadian woods are of the fiercest breed. They border on the wolf. They are called huskies and they are so strong and so fleet of foot that they pull sleds for hours across the frozen lakes at almost the speed of a running horse. It must be confessed that they are handsome and if it happens to be your potato peelings and discarded fish that they eat, they warm into friendliness. Indeed, on these occasions, one can make quite a show of bravery by stroking and dealing lightly with them. But once upon a time in an ignorant moment two other campers and myself followed a lonely railroad track and struck off on a path through the pines in search of a certain trapper on a fur farm. The path went on a broken zigzag avoiding fallen trees and soft hollows, conducting itself on the whole with more patience than firmness. We walked a quarter of a mile, but still we saw no cabin. The line of the railroad had long since disappeared. An eagle wheeled above us and quarrelled at our intrusion. Presently to test our course and learn whether we were coming near the cabin, we gave a shout. Immediately out of the deeper woods there came a clamor that froze us. Such sounds, it seemed, could issue only from bloody and dripping jaws. In a panic, as by a common impulse we turned and ran. Yet we did not run frankly as when the circus lion is loose, but in a shamefaced manner—an attempt at a retreat in good order—something between a walk and a run. At the end of a hundred yards we stopped. No dogs had fallen on us. Danger had not burst its kennel. We hallooed again, to rouse the trapper. At last, after a minute of suspense, came his answering voice, the sweetest sound to be imagined. Whereupon I came down from my high stump which I had climbed for a longer view.

I am convinced that I am not alone in my—shall I say diffidence?—toward dogs. Indeed, there is evidence from the oldest times that mankind, in its more honest moments, has confessed to a fear of dogs. In recognition of this general fear, the unmuzzled Cerberus was put at the gate of Hades. It was rightly felt that when the unhappy pilgrims got within, his fifty snapping heads were better than a bolt upon the door. It was better for them to endure the ills they had, than be nipped in the upper passage. He, also, who first spoke the ancient proverb, *Let sleeping dogs lie*, did no more than voice the caution of the street. And he, also, who invented the saying that the world is going to the bow-wows, lodged his deplorable pessimism in fitting words.

It was Daniel who sat with the lions. But there are degrees of bravery. On Long Street, within sight of my window—just where the street gets into its most tangled traffic—there has hung for many years the painted signboard of a veterinary surgeon. Its artist was in the first flourish of youth. Old age had not yet chilled him when he mixed his gaudy colors. The surgeon's name is set up in modest letters, but the horse below flames with color. What a flaring nostril! What an eager eye! How arched the neck! Here is a wrath and speed unknown to the quadrupeds of this present Long Street. Such mild-eyed, accumbent, sharp-ribbed horses as now infest the curb—mere whittlings from a larger age—hang their heads at their degeneracy. Indeed, these horses seem to their owners not to be worth the price of a nostrum. If disease settles in them, let them lean against a post until the fit is past! And of a consequence, the doctor's work has fallen off. It has become a rare occasion when it is permitted him to stroke his chin in contemplation of some inner palsy. Therefore to give his wisdom scope, the doctor some time since announced the cellar of the building to be a hospital for dogs. Must I press the analogy? I have seen the doctor with bowl and spoon in hand take leave of the cheerful world. He opens the cellar door. A curdling yelp comes up the stairs. In the abyss below there are twenty dogs at least, all of them sick, all dangerous. Not since Orion led his hunting pack across the heavens has there been so fierce a sound. The door closes. There is a final yelp, such as greets a bone. Doubtless, by this time, they are munching on the doctor. Good sir, had you lived in pre-apostolic days, your name would have been lined with Daniel's in the hymn. I might have spent my earliest treble in your praise.

But there are other kinds of dogs. Gentlest of readers, have you ever passed a few days at Tunbridge Wells? It lies on one of the roads that run from London to the Channel and for several hundred years persons have gone there to take the waters against the more fashionable ailments. Its chief fame was in the days when rich folk, to ward off for the season a touch of ancestral gout, travelled down from London in their coaches. We may fancy Lord Thingumdo crossing his sleek legs inside or putting his head to the window on the change of horses. He has outriders and a horn to sound his coming. His Lordship has a liver that must be mended, but also he has a weakness for the gaming table. Or Lady Euphemia, wrapped in silks, languishes mornings in her lodgings with a latest novel, but goes forth at noon upon the Pantilles to shop in the stalls. A box of patches must be bought. A lace flounce has caught her eye. Bless her dear eyes, as she bends upon her purchase she is fair to look upon. The Grand Rout is set for tonight. Who knows but that the Duke will put the tender question and will ask her to name the happy day?

But these golden days are past. Tunbridge Wells has sunk from fashion. The gaming tables are gone. A band still plays mornings in the Pantilles—or did so before the war—but cheaper gauds are offered in the shops. Emerald brooches are fallen to paste. In all the season there is scarcely a single demand for a diamond garter. If there were now a Rout, the only dancers would be stiff shadows from the past. The healing waters still trickle from the ground and an old woman serves you for a penny, but the miracle has gone. The old world is cured and dead.

Tunbridge Wells is visited now chiefly by old ladies whose husbands—to judge by the black lace caps—have left Lombard Street for heaven. At the hotel where I stopped, which was at the top of the Commons outside the thicker town, I was the only man in the breakfast room. Two widows, each with a tiny dog on a chair beside her, sat at the next table. This was their conversation:

"Did you hear her last night?"

"Was it Flossie that I heard?"

"Yes. The poor dear was awake all night. She got her feet wet yesterday when I let her run upon the grass."

But after breakfast—if the day is sunny and the wind sits in a favoring quarter—one by one the widows go forth in their chairs. These are wicker contrivances that hang between three wheels. Burros pull them, and men walk alongside to hold their bridles. Down comes the widow. Down comes a maid with her wraps. Down comes a maid with Flossie. The wraps are adjusted. The widow is handed in. Her feet are wound around with comforters against a draft. Her salts rest in her lap. Her ample bag of knitting is safe aboard. Flossie is placed beside her. Proot! The donkey starts.

All morning the widow sits in the Pantilles and listens to the band and knits. Flossie sits on the flagging at her feet with an intent eye upon the ball of worsted. Twice in a morning—three times if the gods are kind—the ball rolls to the pavement. Flossie has been waiting so long for this to happen. It is the bright moment of her life—the point and peak of happiness. She darts upon it. She paws it exultantly for a moment. Brief is the rainbow and brief the Borealis. The finger of Time is swift.

The poppy blooms and fades. The maid captures the ball of worsted and restores it.

It lies in the widow's lap. The band plays. The needles click to a long tune. The healing waters trickle from the ground. The old woman whines their merits. Flossie sits motionless, her head cocked and her eye upon the ball. Perhaps the god of puppies will again be good to her.

ROADS OF MORNING

My grandfather's farm lay somewhere this side of the sunset, so near that its pastures barely missed the splash of color. But from the city it was a two hours' journey by horse and phaeton. My grandfather drove. I sat next, my feet swinging clear of the lunchbox. My brother had the outside, a place denied to me for fear that I might fall across the wheel. When we were all set, my mother made a last dab at my nose—an unheeded smudge having escaped my vigilance. Then my grandfather said, "Get up,"—twice, for the lazy horse chose to regard the first summons as a jest. We start. The great wheels turn. My brother leans across the guard to view the miracle. We crunch the gravel. We are alive for excitement. My brother plays we are a steamboat and toots. I toot in imitation, but higher up as if I were a younger sort of steamboat. We hold our hands on an imaginary wheel and steer. We scorn grocery carts and all such harbor craft. We are on a long cruise. Street lights will guide us sailing home.

Of course there were farms to the south of the city and apples may have ripened there to as fine a flavor, and to the east, also, doubtless there were farms. It would be asking too much that the west should have all the haystacks, cherry trees and cheese houses. If your judgment skimmed upon the surface, you would even have found the advantage with the south. It was prettier because more rolling. It was shaggier. The country to the south tipped up to the hills, so sharply in places that it might have made its living by collecting nickels for the slide. Indeed, one might think that a part of the city had come bouncing down the slope, for now it lay resting at the bottom, sprawled somewhat for its ease. Or it might appear—if your belief runs on discarded lines—that the whole flat-bottomed earth had been fouled in its celestial course and now lay aslant upon its beam with its cargo shifted and spilled about.

The city streets that led to the south, which in those days ended in lanes, popped out of sight abruptly at the top of the first ridge. And when the earth caught up again with their level, already it was dim and purple and tall trees were no more than a roughened hedge. But what lay beyond that range of hills—what towns and cities—what oceans and forests—how beset with adventure—how fearful after dark—these things you could not see, even if you climbed to some high place and strained yourself on tiptoe. And if you walked from breakfast to lunch—until you gnawed within and were but a hollow drum—there would still be a higher range against the sky. There are misty kingdoms on this whirling earth, but the ways are long and steep.

The lake lay to the north with no land beyond, the city to the east. But to the west—

Several miles outside the city as it then was, and still beyond its clutches, the country was cut by a winding river bottom with sharp edges of shale. Down this valley Rocky River came brawling in the spring, over-fed and quarrelsome. Later in the year—its youthful appetite having caught an indigestion—it shrunk and wasted to a shadow. By August you could cross it on the stones. The uproar of its former flood was marked upon the shale and trunks of trees here and there were wedged, but now the river plays drowsy tunes upon the stones. There is scarcely enough movement of water to flick the sunlight. A leaf on its idle current is a lazy craft whose skipper nods. There were hickory trees on the point above. May-apples grew in the deep woods, and blackberries along the fences. And in the season sober horses plowed up and down the fields with nodding heads, affirming their belief in the goodness of the soil and their willingness to help in its fruition.

Yet the very core of this valley in days past was a certain depth of water at a turn of the stream. There was a clay bank above it and on it small naked boys stood and daubed themselves. One of them put a band of clay about himself by way of decoration. Another, by a more general smudge, made himself a Hottentot and thereby gave his manners a wider scope and license. But by daubing yourself entire you became an Indian and might vent yourself in hideous yells, for it was amazing how the lungs grew stouter when the clay was laid on thick. Then you tapped your flattened palm rapidly against your mouth and released an intermittent uproar in order that the valley might he warned of the deviltry to come. You circled round and round and beat upon the ground in the likeness of a war dance. But at last, sated with scalps, off you dived into the pool and came up a white man. Finally, you stood on one leg and jounced the water from your ear, or pulled a bloodsucker from your toes before he sapped your life—for this tiny creature of the rocks was credited with the gift of prodigious inflation, and might inhale you, blood, sinews, suspenders and all, if left to his ugly purpose.

Farms should not be too precisely located; at least this is true of farms which, like my grandfather's, hang in a mist of memory. I read once of a wonderful spot—quite inferior, doubtless, to my grandfather's farm—which was located by evil directions intentionally to throw a seeker off. Munchausen, you will recall, in the placing of his magic countries, was not above this agreeable villainy. Robinson Crusoe was loose and vague in the placing of his island. It is said that Izaak Walton waved a hand obscurely toward the stream where he had made a catch, but could not be cornered to a nice direction, lest his pool be overrun. In early youth, I myself went, on a mischievous hint, to explore a remote region which I was told lay in the dark behind the kindling pile. But because I moved in a fearful darkness, quite beyond the pale light from the furnace room, I lost the path. It did not lead me to the peaks and the roaring waters.

But the farm was reached by more open methods. Dolly and the phaeton were the chief instruments. First—if you were so sunk in ignorance as not to know the road—you inquired of everybody for the chewing gum factory, to be known by its smell of peppermint. Then you sought the high bridge over the railroad tracks. Beyond was Kamm's Corners. Here, at a turn of the road, was a general store whose shelves sampled the produce of this whole fair world and the factories thereof. One might have thought that the proprietor emulated Noah at the flood by bidding two of each created things to find a place inside.

Beyond Kamm's Corners you came to the great valley. When almost down the hill you passed a house with broken windows and unkept grass. This house, by report, was haunted, but you could laugh at such tales while the morning sun was up. At the bottom of the hill a bridge crossed the river, with loose planking that rattled as though the man who made nails was dead.

Beyond the bridge, at the first rise of ground, the horse stopped — for I assume that you drove a sagacious animal — by way of hint that every one of sound limb get out and walk to the top of the hill. A suspicious horse turned his head now and again and cast his eye upon the buggy to be sure that no one climbed in again.

Presently you came to the toll-gate at the top and paid its keeper five cents, or whatever large sum he demanded. Then your grandfather — if by fortunate chance you happened to have one — asked after his wife and children, and had they missed the croup; then told him his corn was looking well.

My grandfather — for it is time you knew him — lived with us. Because of a railway accident fifteen years before in which one of his legs was cut off just below the knee, he had retired from public office. Several years of broken health had been followed by years that were for the most part free from suffering. My own first recollection reverts to these better years. I recall a tall man — to my eyes a giant, for he was taller even than my father — who came into the nursery as I was being undressed. There was a wind in the chimney, and the windows rattled. He put his crutches against the wall. Then taking me in his arms, he swung me aloft to his shoulder by a series of somersaults. I cried this first time, but later I came to demand the performance.

Once, when I was a little older, I came upon one of his discarded wooden legs as I was playing in the garret of the house. It was my first acquaintance with such a contrivance. It lay behind a pile of trunks and I was, at the time, on my way to the center of the earth, for the cheerful path dove into darkness behind the chimney. You may imagine my surprise. I approached it cautiously. I viewed it from all sides by such dusty light as fell between the trunks. Not without fear I touched it. It was unmistakably a leg — but whose? Was it possible that there was a kind of Bluebeard in the family, who, for his pleasure, lopped off legs? There had been no breath of such a scandal. Yet, if my reading and studies were correct, such things had happened in other families not very different from ours; not in our own town maybe, but in such near-by places as Kandahar and Serendib—places which in my warm regard were but as suburbs to our street, to be gained if you persevered for a hundred lamp-posts. Or could the leg belong to Annie the cook? Her nimbleness with griddle-cakes belied the thought: And once, when the wind had swished her skirts, manifestly she was whole and sound. Then all at once I knew it to be my grandfather's. Grown familiar, I pulled it to the window. I tried it on, but made bad work of walking.

To the eye my grandfather had two legs all the way down and, except for his crutches and an occasional squeak, you would not have detected his infirmity. Evidently the maker did no more than imitate nature, although, for myself, I used to wonder at the poverty of his invention. There would be distinction in a leg, which in addition to its usual functions, would also bend forward at the knee, or had a surprising sidewise joint—and there would be profit, too, if one cared to make a show of it. The greatest niggard on the street would pay two pins for such a sight.

As my grandfather was the only old gentleman of my acquaintance, a wooden leg seemed the natural and suitable accompaniment of old age. Persons, it appeared, in their riper years, cast off a leg, as trees dropped their leaves. But my grandmother puzzled me. Undeniably she retained both of hers, yet her hair was just as white, and she was almost as old. Evidently this law of nature worked only with men. Ladies, it seemed, were not deciduous. But how the amputation was effected in men—whether by day or night—how the choice fell between the right and left—whether the wooden leg came down the chimney (a proper entrance)—how soon my father would go the way of all masculine flesh and cast his off—these matters I could not solve. The Arabian Nights were silent on the subject. Aladdin's uncle, apparently, had both his legs. He was too brisk in villainy to admit a wooden leg. But then, he was only an uncle. If his history ran out to the end, doubtless he would go with a limp in his riper days. The story of the Bible—although it trafficked in such veterans as Methuselah—gave not a hint. Abraham died full of years. Here would have been a proper test—but the book was silent.

My grandfather in those days had much leisure time. He still kept an office at the rear of the house, although he had given up the regular practice of the law. But a few old clients lingered on, chiefly women who carried children in their arms and old men without neckties who came to him for free advice. These he guided patiently in their troubles, and he would sit an hour to listen to a piteous story. In an extremity he gave them money, or took a well-meant but worthless note. Often his callers overran the dinner hour and my mother would have to jingle the dinner bell at the door to rouse them. Occasionally he would be called on for a public speech, and for several days he would be busy at his desk. Frequently he presided at dinners and would tell a story and sing a song, for he had a fine bass voice and was famous for his singing.

He read much in those last years in science. When he was not reading Trowbridge to his grandchildren, it was Huxley to himself. But when his eyes grew tired, he would on an occasion—if there was canning in the house—go into the kitchen where my mother and grandmother worked, and help pare the fruit. Seriously, as though he were engaged upon a game, he would cut the skin into thinnest strips, unbroken to the end, and would hold up the coil for us to see. Or if he broke it in the cutting it was a point against him in the contest.

His diversion rather than his profit was the care and rental of about twenty small houses, some of which he built to fit his pensioners. My brother and myself often made the rounds with him in the phaeton. At most of the houses he was affectionately greeted as "Jedge" and was held in long conversations across the fence. And to see an Irishman was to see a friend. They all knew him and said, "Good mornin'," as we passed. He and they were good Democrats together.

I can see in memory a certain old Irishman in a red flannel shirt, with his foot upon the hub, bending across the wheel and gesticulating in an endless discussion of politics or crops, while my brother and I were impatient to be off. Dolly was of course patient, for she had long since passed her fretful youth. If by any biological chance it had happened that she had been an old lady instead of a horse, she would have been the kind that spent her day in a rocker with her knitting. Any one who gave Dolly an excuse for standing was her friend. There she stood as though she wished the colloquy to last forever.

It was seldom that Dolly lost her restraint. She would, indeed, when she came near the stable, somewhat hasten her stride; and when we came on our drives to the turning point and at last headed about for home, Dolly would know it and show her knowledge by a quickening of the ears and the quiver of a faint excitement. Yet Dolly lost her patience when there were flies. Then she threw off all repression and so waved her tail that she regularly got it across the reins. This stirred my grandfather to something not far short of anger. How vigorously would he try to dislodge the reins by pulling and jerking! Dolly only clamped down her tail the harder. Experience showed that the only way was to go slowly and craftily and without heat or temper—a slackening of the reins—a distraction of Dolly's attention—a leaning across the dashboard—a firm grasping of the tail out near the end—a sudden raising thereof. Ah! It was done. We all settled back against the cushions. Or perhaps a friendly fly would come to our assistance and Dolly would have to use her tail in another direction.

The whip was seldom used. Generally it stood in its socket. It was ornamental like a flagstaff. It forgot its sterner functions. But Dolly must have known the whip in some former life, for even a gesture toward the socket roused her. If it was rattled she mended her pace for a block. But if on a rare occasion my grandfather took it in his hand, Dolly lay one ear back in our direction, for she knew then he meant business. And what an excitement would arise in the phaeton! We held on tight for fear that she might take it into her mild old head to run away.

But Dolly had her moments. One sunny summer afternoon while she grazed peacefully in the orchard, with her reins wound around the whip handle—the appropriate place on these occasions—she was evidently stung by a bee. My brother was at the time regaling himself in a near-by blackberry thicket. He looked up at an unusual sound. Without warning, Dolly had leaped to action and was tearing around the orchard dragging the phaeton behind her. She wrecked the top on a low hanging branch, then hit another tree, severing thereby all connection between herself and the phaeton, and at last galloped down the lane to the farm house, with the broken shafts and harness dangling behind her. Kipling's dun "with the mouth of a bell and the heart of Hell and the head of the gallows-tree," could hardly have shown more spirit. It was as though one brief minute of a glorious youth had come back to her. It was a last spurting of an old flame before it sunk to ash.

My grandfather gave his leisure to his grandchildren. He carved for us with his knife, with an especial knack for willow whistles. He showed us the colors that lay upon the world when we looked at it through one of the glass pendants of the parlor chandelier. He sat by us when we played duck-on-the-rock. He helped us with our kites and gave a superintendence to our toys. It is true that he was superficial with tin-tags and did not know the difference in value between a Steam Engine tag—the rarest of them all—and a common Climax, but we forgave him as one forgives a friend who is ignorant of Persian pottery. He employed us as gardeners and put a bounty on weeds. We watered the lawn together, turn by turn. When I was no more than four years old, he taught us to play casino with him—and afterwards bezique. How he cried out if he got a royal sequence! With what excitement he announced a double bezique! Or if one of us seemed about to score and lacked but a single card, how intently he contended for the last few tricks to thwart our declaration! And if we got it despite his lead of aces, how gravely he squinted on the cards against deception, with his glasses forward on his nose!

When he took his afternoon nap and lay upon his back on the sofa in the sitting-room, we made paper pin-wheels to see whether his breath would stir them. This trick having come to his notice by a sudden awakening, he sometimes thereafter played to be asleep and snored in such a mighty gust that the wheels spun. He was like a Dutch tempest against a windmill.

If a Dime Museum came to town we made an afternoon of it. He took us to all the circuses and gave us our choice of side-shows. We walked up and down before the stretches of painted canvas, balancing in our desire a sword-swallower against an Indian Princess. Most of the fat women and all the dwarfs that I have known came to my acquaintance when in company with my grandfather. As a young man, it was said, he once ran away from home to join a circus as an acrobat, having acquired the trick of leaping upon a running horse. I fancy that his knack of throwing us to his shoulder by a double somersault was a recollection of his early days. You may imagine with what awe we looked on him even though he now went on crutches. He was the epitome of adventure, the very salt of excitement. It was better having him than a pirate in the house. When the circus had gone and life was drab, he was our tutor in the art of turning cart-wheels and making hand-stands against the door.

And once, when we were away from him, he walked all morning about the garden and in his loneliness he gathered into piles the pebbles that we had dropped.

I was too young to know my grandfather in his active days when he was prominent in public matters. His broader abilities are known to others. But though more than twenty years have passed since his death, I remember his tone of voice, his walk, his way of handling a crutch, all his tricks of speech and conduct as though he had just left the room. And I can think of nothing more beautiful than that a useful man who has faced the world for seventy years and has done his part, should come back in his old age to the nursery and be the playfellow of his grandchildren.

But the best holiday was a trip to the farm.

This farm—to which in our slow trot we have been so long a time in coming—lay for a mile on the upper land, and its grain fields and pastures looked down into the valley. The buildings, however, were set close to the road and fixed their interest on such occasional wagons as creaked by. A Switzer occupied the farm, who owned, in addition to the more immediate members of his family, a cuckoo clock whose weights hung on long cords which by Saturday night reached almost to the floor. When I have sat at his table, I have neglected cheese and the lesser foods, when the hour came near, in order not to miss the cuckoo's popping out. And in the duller spaces, when the door was shut, I have fancied it sitting in the dark and counting the minutes to itself.

The Switzer's specialty was the making of a kind of rubber cheese which one could learn to like in time. Of the processes of its composition, I can remember nothing except that when it was in the great press the whey ran from its sides, but this may be common to all cheeses. I was once given a cup of this whey to drink and I brightened, for until it was in my mouth, I thought it was buttermilk. Beyond was the spring-house with cans of milk set in the cool water and with a trickling sound beneath the boards. From the spring-house there started those mysterious cow-paths that led down into the great gorge that cut the farm. Here were places so deep that only a bit of the sky showed and here the stones were damp. It was a place that seemed to lie nearer to the confusion when the world was made, and rocks lay piled as though a first purpose had been broken off. And to follow a cow-path, regardless of where it led, was, in those days, the essence of hazard; though all the while from the pastures up above there came the flat safe tinkling of the bells.

The apple orchard—where Dolly was stung by the bee—was set on a fine breezy place at the brow of the hill with the valley in full sight. The trees themselves were old and decayed, but they were gnarled and crotched for easy climbing. And the apples—in particular a russet—mounted to a delicacy. On the other side of the valley, a half mile off as a bird would fly, were the buildings of a convent, and if you waited you might hear the twilight bell. To this day all distant bells come to my ears with a pleasing softness, as though they had been cast in a quieter world. Stone arrow-heads were found in a near-by field as often as the farmer turned up the soil in plowing. And because of this, a long finger of land that put off to the valley, was called Indian Point. Here, with an arm for pillow, one might lie for a long hour on a sunny morning and watch the shadows of clouds move across the lowland. A rooster crows somewhere far off—surely of all sounds the drowsiest. A horse in a field below lifts up its head and neighs. The leaves practice a sleepy tune. If one has the fortune to keep awake, here he may lie and think the thoughts that are born of sun and wind.

And now, although it is not yet noon, hunger rages in us. The pancakes, the syrup, the toast and the other incidents of breakfast have disappeared the way the rabbit vanishes when the magician waves his hand. The horrid Polyphemus did not so crave his food. And as yet there is no comforting sniff from the kitchen. Scrubbing and other secular matters engage the farmer's wife. There is as yet not a faintest gurgle in the kettle.

To divert ourselves, we climb three trees and fall out of one. Is twelve o'clock never to come? Have Time and the Hour grown stagnant? We eat apples and throw the cores at the pig to hear him grunt. Is the great round sun stuck? Have the days of Joshua come again? We walk a rail fence. Is it not yet noon? Shrewsbury clock itself—reputed by scholars the slowest of all possible clocks—could not so hold off. I snag myself—but it is nothing that shows when I sit.

Ah! At last! My grandfather is calling from the house. We run back and find that the lunch is ready and is laid upon a table with a red oil-cloth cover. We apply ourselves. Silence….

The journey home started about five o'clock. There was one game we always played. Each of us, having wisely squinted at the sky, made a reckoning and guessed where we would be when the sun set. My grandfather might say the high bridge. I named the Sherman House. But my brother, being precise, judged it to a fraction of a telegraph pole. Beyond a certain turn—did we remember?—well, it would be exactly sixteen telegraph poles further on. What an excitement there was when the sun's lower rim was already below the horizon! We stood on our knees and looked through the little window at the back of the phaeton. With what suspicion we regarded my grandfather's driving! Or if Dolly lagged, did it not raise a thought that she, too, was in the plot against us? The sun sets. We cry out the victor.

The sky flames with color. Then deadens in the east. The dusk is falling. The roads grow dark. Where run the roads of night? While there is light, you can see the course they keep across the country—the dust of horses' feet—a bridge—a vagrant winding on a hill beyond. All day long they are busy with the feet of men and women and children shouting. Then twilight comes, and the roads lead home to supper and the curling smoke above the roof. But at night where run the roads? It's dark beyond the candle's flare—where run the roads of night.

My brother and I have become sleepy. We lop over against my grandfather—

We awake with a start. There is a gayly lighted horse-car jingling beside us. The street lights show us into harbor. We are home at last.

The Man Of Grub Street Comes From His Garret

I have come to live this winter in New York City and by good fortune I have found rooms on a pleasant park. This park, which is but one block in extent, is so set off from the thoroughfares that it bears chiefly the traffic that is proper to the place itself. Grocery carts jog around and throw out their wares. Laundry wagons are astir. A little fat tailor on an occasion carries in an armful of newly pressed clothing with suspenders hanging. Dogs are taken out to walk but are held in leash, lest a taste of liberty spoil them for an indoor life. The center of the park is laid out with grass and trees and pebbled paths, and about it is a high iron fence. Each house has a key to the enclosure. Such social infection, therefore, as gets inside the gates is of our own breeding. In the sunny hours nurses and children air themselves in this grass plot. Here a gayly painted wooden velocipede is in fashion. At this minute there are several pairs of fat legs a-straddle this contrivance. It is a velocipede as it was first made, without pedals. Beau Brummel—for the velocipede dates back to him—may have walked forth to take the waters at Tunbridge Wells on a vehicle not far different, but built to his greater stature. There is also a trickle of drays and wagons across the park—a mere leakage from the streets, as though the near-by traffic in the pressure had burst its pipes. But only at morning and night when the city collects or discharges its people, are the sidewalks filled. Then for a half hour the nozzle of the city plays a full stream on us.

The park seems to be freer and more natural than the streets outside. A man goes by gesticulating as though he practiced for a speech. A woman adjusts her stocking on the coping below the fence with the freedom of a country road. A street sweeper, patched to his office, tunes his slow work to fit the quiet surroundings. Boys skate by or cut swirls upon the pavement in the privilege of a play-ground.

My work—if anything so pleasant and unforced can carry the name—is done at a window that overlooks this park. Were it not for several high buildings in my sight I might fancy that I lived in one of the older squares of London. There is a look of Thackeray about the place as though the Osbornes might be my neighbors. A fat man who waddles off his steps opposite, if he would submit to a change of coat, might be Jos Sedley starting for his club to eat his chutney. If only there were a crest above my bell-pull I might even expect Becky Sharp in for tea. Or occasionally I divert myself with the fancy that I am of a still older day and that I have walked in from Lichfield—I choose the name at hazard—with a tragedy in my pocket, to try my fortune. Were it not for the fashion of dress in the park below and some remnant of reason in myself, I could, in a winking moment, persuade myself that my room is a garret and my pen a quill. On such delusion, before I issued on the street to seek my coffee-house, I would adjust my wig and dust myself of snuff.

But for my exercise and recreation—which for a man of Grub Street is necessary in the early hours of afternoon when the morning fires have fallen—I go outside the park. I have a wide choice for my wanderings. I may go into the district to the east and watch the children play against the curb. If they pitch pennies on the walk I am careful to go about, for fear that I distract the throw. Or if the stones are marked for hop-scotch, I squeeze along the wall. It is my intention—from which as yet my diffidence withholds me—to present to the winner of one of these contests a red apple which I shall select at a corner stand. Or an ice wagon pauses in its round, and while the man is gone there is a pleasant thieving of bits of ice. Each dirty cheek is stuffed as though a plague of mumps had fallen on the street. Or there may be a game of baseball—a scampering on the bases, a home-run down the gutter—to engage me for an inning. Or shinny grips the street. But if a street organ comes—not a mournful one-legged box eked out with a monkey, but a big machine with an extra man to pull—the children leave their games. It was but the other day that I saw six of them together dancing on the pavement to the music, with skirts and pigtails flying. There was such gladness in their faces that the musician, although he already had his nickel, gave them an extra tune. It was of such persuasive gayety that the number of dancers at once went up to ten and others wiggled to the rhythm. And for myself, although I am past my sportive days, the sound of a street organ, if any, would inflame me to a fox-trot. Even a surly tune — if the handle be quickened — comes from the box with a brisk seduction. If a dirge once got inside, it would fret until it came out a dancing measure.

In this part of town, on the better streets, I sometimes study the fashions as I see them in the shops and I compare them with those of uptown stores. Nor is there the difference one might suppose. The small round muff that sprang up this winter in the smarter shops won by only a week over the cheaper stores. Tan gaiters ran a pretty race. And I am now witness to a dead heat in a certain kind of fluffy rosebud dress. The fabrics are probably different, but no matter how you deny it, they are cut to a common pattern.

In a poorer part of the city still nearer to the East River, where smells of garlic and worse issue from cellarways, I came recently on a considerable park. It was supplied with swings and teeters and drew children on its four fronts. Of a consequence the children of many races played together. I caught a Yiddish answer to an Italian question. I fancy that a child here could go forth at breakfast wholly a Hungarian and come home with a smack of Russian or Armenian added. The general games that merged the smaller groups, aided in the fusion. If this park is not already named — a small chance, for it shows the marks of age — it might properly be called *The Park of the Thirty Nations.*

Or my inclination may take me to the lower city. Like a poor starveling I wander in the haunts of wealth where the buildings are piled to forty stories, and I spin out the ciphers in my brain in an endeavor to compute the amount that is laid up inside. Also, lest I become discontented with my poverty, I note the strain and worry of the faces that I meet. There is a story of Tolstoi in which a man is whispered by his god that he may possess such land as he can circle in a day. Until that time he had been living on a fertile slope of sun and shadow, with fields ample for his needs. But when the whisper came, at a flash, he pelted off across the hills. He ran all morning, but as the day advanced his sordid ambition broadened and he turned his course into a wider and still wider circle. Here a pleasant valley tempted him and he bent his path to bring it inside his mark. Here a fruitful upland led him off. As the day wore on he ran with a greater fierceness, because he knew he would lose everything if he did not reach his starting place before the sun went down. The sun was coming near the rim of earth when he toiled up the last hill. His feet were cut by stones, his face pinched with agony. He staggered toward the goal and fell across it while as yet there was a glint of light. But his effort burst his heart. Does the analogy hold on these narrow streets? To a few who sit in an inner office, Mammon has made a promise of wealth and domination. These few run breathless to gain a mountain. But what have the gods whispered to the ten thousand who sit in the outer office, that they bend and blink upon their ledgers? Have the gods whispered to them the promise of great wealth? Alas, before them there lies only the dust and heat of a level road, yet they too are broken at the sunset.

Less oppressive are the streets where commerce is more apparent. Here, unless you would be smirched, it is necessary to walk fast and hold your coat-tails in. Packing cases are going down slides. Bales are coming up in hoists. Barrels are rolling out of wagons. Crates are being lifted in. Is the exchange never to stop? Is no warehouse satisfied with what it has? English, which until now you judged a soft concordant language, shows here its range and mastery of epithet. And all about, moving and jostling the boxes, are men with hooks. One might think that in a former day Captain Cuttle had settled here to live and that his numerous progeny had kept the place.

Often I ride on a bus top like a maharajah on an elephant, up near the tusks, as it were, where the view is unbroken. I plan this trip so that I move counter to the procession that goes uptown in the late afternoon. Is there a scene like it in the world? The boulevards of Paris in times of peace are hardly so gay. Fifth Avenue is blocked with motor cars. Fashion has gone forth to select a feather. A ringlet has gone awry and must be mended. The Pomeranian's health is served by sunlight. The Spitz must have an airing. Fashion has wagged its head upon a Chinese vase—has indeed squinted at it through a lorgnette against a fleck—and now lolls home to dinner. Or style has veered an inch, and it has been a day of fitting. At restaurant windows one may see the feeding of the over-fed. Men sit in club windows and still wear their silk hats as though there was no glass between them and the windy world. Footmen in boots and breeches sit as stiffly as though they were toys grown large and had metal spikes below to hold them to their boxes. They look like the iron firemen that ride on nursery fire-engines. For all these sights the bus top is the best place.

And although we sit on a modest roof, the shopkeepers cater to us. For in many of the stores, is there not an upper tier of windows for our use? The commodities of this second story are quite as fine as those below. And the waxen beauties who display the frocks greet us in true democracy with as sweet a simper.

My friend G— — while riding recently on a bus top met with an experience for which he still blushes.

There was a young woman sitting directly in front of him, and when he came to leave, a sudden lurch threw him against her. When he recovered his footing, which was a business of some diffi-culty, for the bus pitched upon a broken pavement, what was his chagrin to find that a front button of his coat had hooked in her back hair! Luckily G— — was not seized with a panic. Rather, he labored cautiously—but without result. Nor could she help in the disentanglement. Their embarrassment might have been indefinite-ly prolonged—indeed, G— — was several blocks already down the street—when he bethought him of his knife and so cut off the but-ton. As he pleasantly expressed it to the young woman, he would give her the choice of the button or the coat entire.

Reader, are you inclined toward ferry boats? I cannot include those persons who journey on them night and morning perfunctori-ly. These persons keep their noses in their papers or sit snugly in the cabin. If the market is up, they can hardly be conscious even that they are crossing a river. Nor do I entirely blame them. If one kept shop on a breezy tip of the Delectable Mountains with all the re-gions of the world laid out below, he could not be expected to climb up for the hundredth time with a first exhilaration, or to swing his alpenstock as though he were on a rare holiday. If one had business across the Styx too often—although the scenery on its banks is re-puted to be unusual—he might in time sit below and take to yawning. Father Charon might have to jog his shoulder to rouse him when the boat came between the further piers.

But are you one of those persons who, not being under a daily compulsion, rides upon a ferry boat for the love of the trip? Being in this class myself, I laid my case the other night before the gateman, and asked his advice regarding routes. He at once entered sympathetically into my distemper and gave me a plan whereby with but a single change of piers I might at an expense of fourteen cents cross the river four times at different angles.

It was at the end of day and a light fog rested on the water. Nothing was entirely lost, yet a gray mystery wrapped the ships and buildings. If New Jersey still existed it was dim and shadowy as though its real life had gone and but a ghost remained. Ferry boats were lighted in defiance of the murk, and darted here and there at reckless angles. An ocean liner was putting out, and several tugs had rammed their noses against her sides. There is something engaging about a tug. It snorts with eagerness. It kicks and splashes. It bursts itself to lend a hand. And how it butts with its nose! Surely its forward cartilages are of triple strength, else in its zest it would jam its nasal passages.

Presently we came opposite lower New York. Although the fog concealed the outlines of the buildings, their lights showed through. This first hour of dark is best, before the day's work is done and while as yet all of the windows are lighted. The Woolworth Tower was suffused in a soft and shadowy light. The other buildings showed like mountains of magic pin-pricks. It was as though all the constellations of heaven on a general bidding had met for conference.

The man of Grub Street, having by this time somewhat dispelled the fumes of dullness from his head, descends from his ferry boat and walks to his quiet park. There is a dull roar from the elevated railway on Third Avenue where the last of the day's crowd goes home. The sidewalks are becoming empty. There is a sheen of water on the pavement. In the winter murk there is a look of Thackeray about the place as though the Sedleys or the Osbornes might be his neighbors. If there were a crest above his bell-pull he might even expect Becky Sharp in for tea.

Now that Spring is here

When the sun set last night it was still winter. The persons who passed northward in the dusk from the city's tumult thrust their hands deep into their pockets and walked to a sharp measure. But a change came in the night. The north wind fell off and a breeze blew up from the south. Such stars as were abroad at dawn left off their shrill winter piping—if it be true that stars really sing in their courses—and pitched their voices to April tunes. One star in particular that hung low in the west until the day was up, knew surely that the Spring had come and sang in concert with the earliest birds. There is a dull belief that these early birds shake off their sleep to get the worm. Rather, they come forth at this hour to cock their ears upon the general heavens for such new tunes as the unfaded stars still sing. If an ear is turned down to the rummage of worms in the earth—for to the superficial, so does the attitude attest—it is only that the other ear may be turned upward to catch the celestial harmonies; for birds know that if there is an untried melody in heaven it will sound first across the clear pastures of the dawn. All the chirping and whistling from the fields and trees are then but the practice of the hour. When the meadowlark sings on a fence-rail she but cons her lesson from the stars.

It is on such a bright Spring morning that the housewife, duster in hand, throws open her parlor window and looks upon the street. A pleasant park is below, of the size of a city square, and already it stirs with the day's activity. The housewife beats her cloth upon the sill and as the dust flies off, she hears the cries and noises of the place. In a clear tenor she is admonished that there is an expert hereabouts to grind her knives. A swarthy baritone on a wagon lifts up his voice in praise of radishes and carrots. His eye roves along the windows. The crook of a hungry finger will bring him to a stand. Or a junkman is below upon his business. Yesterday the bells upon his cart would have sounded sour, but this morning they rattle agreeably, as though a brisker cow than common, springtime in her hoofs, were jangling to her pasture. At the sound—if you are of country training—you see yourself, somewhat misty through the years, barefoot in a grassy lane, with stick in hand, urging the gentle beast. There is a subtle persuasion in the junkman's call. In these tones did the magician, bawling for old lamps, beguile Aladdin. If there were this morning in my lodging an unrubbed lamp, I would toss it from the window for such magic as he might extract from it. And if a fair Princess should be missing at the noon and her palace be skipped from sight, it will follow on the rubbing of it.

The call of red cherries in the park—as you might guess from its Italian source—is set to an amorous tune. What lady, smocked in morning cambric, would not be wooed by such a voice? The gay fellow tempts her to a purchase. It is but a decent caution—now that Spring is here—that the rascal does not call his wares by moonlight. As for early peas this morning, it is Pan himself who peddles them—disguised and smirched lest he be caught in the deception— Pan who stamps his foot and shakes the thicket—whose habit is to sing with reedy voice of the green willows that dip in sunny waters. Although he now clatters his tins and baskets and cries out like a merchant, his thoughts run to the black earth and the shady hollows and the sound of little streams.

I have wondered as I have observed the housewives lingering at their windows—for my window also looks upon the park—I have wondered that these melodious street cries are not used generally for calling the wares of wider sale. If a radish can be so proclaimed, there might be a lilt devised in praise of other pleasing merceries—a tripping pizzicato for laces and frippery—a brave trumpeting for some newest cereal. And should not the latest book—if it be a tale of love, for these I am told are best offered to the public in the Spring (sad tales are best for winter)—should not a tale of love be heralded through the city by the singing of a ballad, with a melting tenor in the part? In old days a gaudy rogue cried out upon the broader streets that jugglers had stretched their rope in the market-place, but when the bears came to town, the news was piped even to the narrowest lanes that house-folk might bring their pennies.

With my thoughts set on the Spring I chanced to walk recently where the theatres are thickest. It was on a Saturday afternoon and the walk was crowded with amusement seekers. Presently in the press I observed a queer old fellow carrying on his back a mon- strous pack of umbrellas. He rang a bell monotonously and professed himself a mender of umbrellas. He can hardly have expected to find a customer in the crowd. Even a blinking eye—and these street merchants are shrewd in these matters—must have told him that in all this hurrying mass of people, the thoughts of no one ran toward umbrellas. Rather, I think that he was taking an hour from the routine of the day. He had trod the profitable side streets until truantry had taken him. But he still made a pretext of working at his job and called his wares to ease his conscience from idleness. Once when an unusually bright beam of sunlight fell from between the clouds, he tilted up his hat to get the warmth and I thought him guilty of a skip and syncopation in the ringing of his bell, as if he too twitched pleasantly with the Spring and his old sap was stirred.

I like these persons who ply their trades upon the sidewalk. My hatter—the fellow who cleans my straw hat each Spring—is a partner of a bootblack. Over his head as he putters with his soap and brushes, there hangs a rusty sign proclaiming that he is famous for his cleaning all round the world. He is so modest in his looks that I have wondered whether he really can read the sign. Or perhaps like a true merchant, he is not squeamish at the praise. As I have not previously been aware that any of his profession ever came to general fame except the Mad Hatter of Wonderland, I have squinted sharply at him to see if by chance it might be he, but there are no marks even of a distant kinship. He does, however, bring my hat to a marvellous whiteness and it may be true that he has really tended heads that are now gone beyond Constantinople.

Bootblacks have a sense of rhythm unparalleled. Of this the long rag is their instrument. They draw it once or twice across the shoe to set the key and then they go into a swift and pattering melody. If there is an unusual genius in the bootblack—some remnant of ancient Greece—he plays such a lively tune that one's shoulders jig to it. If there were a dryad or other such nimble creature on the street, she would come leaping as though Orpheus strummed a tune, but the dance is too fast for our languid northern feet.

Nowhere are apples redder than on a cart. Our hearts go out to Adam in the hour of his temptation. I know one lady of otherwise careful appetite who even leans toward dates if she may buy them from a cart. "Those dear dirty dates," she calls them, but I cannot share her liking for them. Although the cart is a beguiling market, dates so bought are too dusty to be eaten. They rank with the apple-john. The apple-john is that mysterious leathery fruit, sold more often from a stand than from a cart, which leans at the rear of the shelf against the peppermint jars. For myself, although I do not eat apple-johns, I like to look at them. They are so shrivelled and so flat, as though a banana had caught a consumption. Or rather, in the older world was there not a custom at a death of sending fruits to support the lonesome journey? If so, the apple-john came untasted to the end. Indeed, there is a look of old Egypt about the fruit. Whether my fondness for gazing at apple-johns springs from a distant occasion when as a child I once bought and ate one, or whether it arises from the fact that Falstaff called Prince Hal a dried apple-john, is an unsolved question, but I like to linger before a particularly shrivelled one and wonder what its youth was like. Perhaps like many of its betters, it remained unheralded and unknown all through its fresher years and not until the coming of its wrinkled age was it at last put up to the common view. The apple-john sets up kinship with an author.

The day of all fools is wisely put in April. The jest of the day resides in the success with which credulity is imposed upon, and April is the month of easiest credulity. Let bragging travellers come in April and hold us with tales of the Anthropopagi! If their heads are said to grow beneath their shoulders, still we will turn a credent ear. Indeed, it is all but sure that Baron Munchausen came back from his travels in the Spring. When else could he have got an ear? What man can look upon the wonders of the returning year—the first blue skies, the soft rains, the tender sproutings of green stalks without feeling that there is nothing beyond belief? If such miracles can happen before his eyes, shall not the extreme range even of travel or metaphysics be allowed? What man who has smelled the first fragrance of the earth, has heard the birds on their northern flight and has seen an April brook upon its course, will withhold his credence even though the jest be plain?

I beg, therefore, that when you walk upon the street on the next day of April fool, that you yield to the occasion. If an urchin points his finger at your hat, humor him by removing it! Look sharply at it for a supposed defect! His glad shout will be your reward. Or if you are begged piteously to lift a stand-pipe wrapped to the likeness of a bundle, even though you sniff the imposture, seize upon it with a will! It is thus, beneath these April skies, that you play your part in the pageantry that marks the day.

The Friendly Genii

Do you not confess yourself to be several years past that time of greenest youth when burnt cork holds its greatest charm? Although not fallen to a crippled state, are you not now too advanced to smudge your upper lip and stalk agreeably as a villain? Surely you can no longer frisk lightly in a comedy. If you should wheeze and limp in an old man's part, with back humped in mimicry, would you not fear that it bordered on the truth? But doubtless there was a time when you ranged upon these heights — when Kazrac the magician was not too heavy for your art. In those soaring days, let us hope that you played the villain with a swagger, or being cast in a softer role, that you won a pink and fluffy princess before the play was done. Your earliest practice, it may be, was in rigging the parlor hangings as a curtain with brown string from the pantry and safety pins. Although you had no show to offer, you said "ding" three times — as is the ancient custom of the stage when the actors are ready — and drew them wide apart. The cat was the audience, who dozed with an ear twitching toward your activity. A complaint that springs up in youth and is known as "snuffles" had kept you out of school. It had gripped you hard at breakfast, when you were sunk in fear of your lessons, but had abated at nine o'clock. Whether the cure came with a proper healing of the nasal glands or followed merely on the ringing of the school bell, must be left to a cool judgment.

Your theatre filled the morning. When Annie came on her quest for dust, you tooted once upon your nose, just to show that a remnant of your infirmity persisted, then put your golden convalescence on the making of your curtain.

But in the early hours of afternoon when the children are once more upon the street, you regret your illness. Here they come trooping by threes and fours, carrying their books tied up in straps. One would think that they were in fear lest some impish fact might get outside the covers to spoil the afternoon. Until the morrow let two and two think themselves five at least! And let Ohio be bounded as it will! Some few children skip ropes, or step carefully across the cracks of the sidewalk for fear they spoil their suppers. Ah!—a bat goes by—a glove—a ball! And now from a vacant lot there comes the clamor of choosing sides. Is no mention to be made of you—you, "molasses fingers"—the star left fielder—the timely batter? What would you not give now for a clean bill of health? You rub your offending nose upon the glass. What matters it with what deep rascality in black mustachios you once strutted upon your boards? What is Hecuba to you?

My own first theatre was in the attic, a place of squeaks and shadows to all except the valiant. In it were low, dark corners where the night crawled in and slept. But in the open part where the roof was highest, there was the theatre. Its walls were made of a red cambric of a flowered pattern that still lingers with me, and was bought with a clatter of pennies on the counter, together with nickels that had escaped my extravagance at the soda fountain.

A cousin and I were joint proprietors. In the making of it, the hammer and nails were mine by right of sex, while she stitched in womanish fashion on the fabrics. She was leading woman and I was either the hero or the villain as fitted to my mood. My younger cousin—although we scorned her for her youth—was admitted to the slighter parts. She might daub herself with cork, but it must be only when we were done. Nor did we allow her to carry the paper knife—shaped like a dagger—which figured hugely in our plots. If we gave her any word to speak, it was as taffy to keep her silent about some iniquity that we had worked against her. In general, we judged her to be too green and giddy for the heavy parts. At the most, she might take pins at the door—for at such a trifle we displayed our talents—or play upon the comb as orchestra before the rising of the curtain.

The usual approach to this theatre was the kitchen door, and those who came to enjoy the drama sniffed at their very entrance the new-baked bread. A pan of cookies was set upon a shelf and a row of apples was ranged along the window sill. Of the ice-box around the corner, not a word, lest hunger lead you off! As for the cook, although her tongue was tart upon a just occasion and although she shooed the children with her apron, secretly she liked to have them crowding through her kitchen.

Now if you, reader—for I assume you to be one of the gathering audience—were of the kind careful on scrubbing days to scrape your feet upon the iron outside and to cross the kitchen on the un-washed parts, then it is likely that you stood in the good graces of the cook. Mark your reward! As you journeyed upward, you munched upon a cookie and bit scallops in its edge. Or if a ravenous haste was in you—as commonly comes up in the middle after-noon—you waived this slower method and crammed yourself with a recklessness that bestrewed the purlieus of your mouth. If your ears lay beyond the muss, the stowage was deemed decent and in order.

Is there not a story in which children are tracked by an ogre through the perilous wood by the crumbs they dropped? Then let us hope there is no ogre lurking on these back stairs, for the trail is plain. It would be near the top, farthest from the friendly kitchen, that the attack might come, for there the stairs yielded to the dark-ness of the attic. There it was best to look sharp and to turn the cor-ners wide. A brave whistling kept out the other noises.

It was after Aladdin had been in town that the fires burned hot-test in us. My grandfather and I went together to the matinee, his great thumb within my fist. We were frequent companions. Togeth-er we had sat on benches in the park and poked the gravel into pat-terns. We went to Dime Museums. Although his eyes had looked longer on the world than mine, we seemed of an equal age.

The theatre was empty as we entered. We carried a bag of candy against a sudden appetite—colt's foot, a penny to the stick. Here and there ushers were clapping down the seats, sounds to my fancy not unlike the first corn within a popper. Somewhere aloft there must have been a roof, else the day would have spied in on us, yet it was lost in the gloom. It was as though a thrifty owner had borrowed the dusky fabrics of the night to make his cover. The curtain was indistinct, but we knew it to be the Stratford Church and we dimly saw its spire.

Now, on the opening of a door to the upper gallery, there was a scampering to get seats in front, speed being whetted by a long half hour of waiting on the stairs. Ghostly, unbodied heads, like the luminous souls of lost mountaineers—for this was the kind of fiction, got out of the Public Library, that had come last beneath my thumb—ghostly heads looked down upon us across the gallery rail.

And now, if you will tip back your head like a paper-hanger—whose Adam's apple would seem to attest a life of sidereal contemplation—you will see in the center of the murk above you a single point of light. It is the spark that will ignite the great gas chandelier. I strain my neck to the point of breaking. My grandfather strains his too, for it is a game between us which shall announce the first spurting of the light. At last! We cry out together. The spark catches the vent next to it. It runs around the circle of glass pendants. The whole blazes up. The mountaineers come to life. They lean forward on their elbows.

From the wings comes the tuning of the violins. A flute ripples up and down in a care-free manner as though the villain Kazrac were already dead and virtue had come into its own. The orchestra emerges from below. Their calmness is but a pretense. Having looked on such sights as lie behind the curtain, having trod such ways, they should be bubbling with excitement. Yet observe the bass viol! How sodden is his eye! How sunken is his gaze! With what dull routine he draws his bow, as though he knew naught but sleepy tunes! If there be any genie in the place, as the program says, let him first stir this sad fellow from his melancholy!

We consult our programs. The first scene is the magician's cave where he plans his evil schemes. The second is the Chinese city where he pretends to be Aladdin's uncle. And for myself, did a friendly old gentleman offer me lollypops and all-day-suckers—for so did the glittering baubles present themselves across the footlights—like Aladdin I, too, would not have squinted too closely on his claim. Gladly I would have gone off with him on an all-day picnic toward the Chinese mountains.

We see a lonely pass in the hills, the cave of jewels (splendid to the eye of childhood) where the slave of the lamp first appears, and finally the throne-room with Aladdin seated safely beside his princess.

Who knows how to dip a pen within the twilight? Who shall trace the figures of the mist? The play is done. We come out in silence. Our candy is but a remnant. Darkness has fallen. The pavements are wet and shining, so that the night might see his face, if by chance the old fellow looked our way.

All about there are persons hurrying home with dinner-pails, who, by their dull eyes, seem never to have heard what wonders follow on the rubbing of a lamp.

But how the fires leaped up—how ambition beat within us—how our attic theatre was wrought to perfection—how the play came off and wracked the neighborhood of its pins—with what grace I myself acted Aladdin—these things must be written by a vain and braggart pen.

Mr. Pepys Sits in the Pit

When it happens that a man has risen to be a member of Parliament, the Secretary of the British Navy and the President of the Royal Society, when he has become the adviser of the King and is moreover the one really bright spot in that King's reign, it is amazing that considerably more than one hundred years after his death, when the navy that he nurtured dominates the seven seas, that he himself on a sudden should be known, not for his larger accomplishments, but as a kind of tavern crony and pot-companion. When he should be standing with fame secure in a solemn though dusty niche in the Temple of Time, it is amazing that he should be remembered chiefly for certain quarrels with his wife and as a frequenter of plays and summer gardens.

Yet this is the fate of Samuel Pepys. Before the return of the Stuarts he held a poor clerkship in the Navy Office and cut his quill obscurely at the common desk. At the Restoration, partly by the boost of influence, but chiefly by his substantial merit, he mounted to several successively higher posts. The Prince of Wales became his friend and patron and when he became Lord High Admiral he took Pepys with him in his advancement. Thus in 1684, Pepys became Secretary of the Navy. When later the Prince of Wales became King James II, Pepys, although his office remained the same, came to quite a pinnacle of administrative power. He was shrewd and capable in the conduct of his position and brought method to the Navy Office. He was a prime factor in the first development of the British Navy. Later victories that were to sweep the seas may be traced in part to him. Nelson rides upon his shoulders. These achievements should have made his fame secure. But on a sudden he gained for posterity a less dignified although a more interesting and enduring renown.

In life, Samuel Pepys walked gravely in majestical robe with full-bottomed wig and with ceremonial lace flapping at his wrists. Every step, if his portrait is to be believed, was a bit of pageantry. Such was his fame, that if his sword but clacked a warning on the pavement, it must have brought the apprentices to the windows. Tradesmen laid down their wares to get a look at him. Fat men puffed and strained to gain the advantage of a sill. Fashionable ladies peeped from brocaded curtains and ogled for his regard. Or if he went by chair, the carriers held their noses up as though offended by the common air. When he spoke before the Commons, the galleries were hushed. He gave his days to the signing of stiff parchments—Admiralty Orders or what not. He checked the King himself at the council table. In short, he was not only a great personage, but also he was quite well aware of the fact and held himself accordingly.

But now many years have passed, and Time, that has so long been at bowls with reputations, has acquired a moderate skill in knocking them down. Let us see how it fares with Pepys! Some men who have been roguish in their lives have been remembered by their higher accomplishments. A string of sonnets or a novel or two, if it catches the fancy, has wiped out a tap-room record. The winning of a battle has obliterated a meanly spent youth. It is true that for a while an old housewife who once lived on the hero's street will shake a dubious finger on his early pranks. Stolen apples or cigarettes behind the barn cram her recollection. But even a village reputation fades. In time the sonnets and glorious battle have the upper place. But things went the other way with Pepys. Rather, his fate is like that of Zeus, who—if legend is to be trusted—was in his life a person of some importance whose nod stirred society on Olympus, but who is now remembered largely for his flirtations and his braggart conduct. A not unlike evil has fallen on the magnificent Mr. Pepys.

This fate came to him because—as the world knows—it happened that for a period of ten years in comparative youth, he wrote an interesting and honest diary. He began this diary in 1659, while he was still a poor clerk living with his wife in a garret, and ended it in 1669, when, although he had emerged from obscurity, his greater honors had not yet been set on him. All the facts of his life during this period are put down, whether good or bad, small or large, generous or mean. He writes of his mornings spent in work at his office, of his consultations with higher officials. There is much running to and fro of business. The Dutch war bulks to a proper length. Parliament sits through a page at a stretch. Pepys goes upon the streets in the days of the plague and writes the horror of it—the houses marked with red crosses and with prayers scratched beneath—the stench and the carrying of dead bodies. He sees the great fire of London from his window on the night it starts; afterwards St. Paul's with its roofs fallen. He is on the fleet that brings Charles home from his long travels, and afterwards when Charles is crowned, he records the processions and the crowds. But also Pepys quarrels with his wife and writes it out on paper. He debauches a servant and makes a note of it. He describes a supper at an ale-house, and how he plays on the flute. He sings "Beauty Retire," a song of his own making, and tells how his listeners "cried it up."

In consequence of this, Samuel Pepys is now known chiefly for his attentions to the pretty actresses of Drury Lane, for kissing Nell

Gwynne in her tiring-room, for his suppers with "the jade" Mrs. Knipp, for his love of a tune upon the fiddle, for coming home from Vauxhall by wherry late at night, "singing merrily" down the river. Or perhaps we recall him best for burying his wine and Parmazan cheese in his garden at the time of the Fire, or for standing to the measure of Mr. Pin the tailor for a "camlett cloak with gold buttons," or for sitting for his portrait in an Indian gown which he "hired to be drawn in." Who shall say that this is not the very portrait by which we have fancied him stalking off to Commons? Could the apprentices have known in what a borrowed majesty he walked, would they not have tossed their caps in mirth and pointed their dusky fingers at him?

Or we remember that he once lived in a garret, and that his wife, "poor wretch," was used to make the fire while Samuel lay abed, and that she washed his "foul clothes"—that by degrees he came to be wealthy and rode in his own yellow coach—that his wife went abroad in society "in a flowered tabby gown"—that Pepys forsook his habits of poverty and exchanged his twelve-penny seat in the theatre gallery for a place in the pit—and that on a rare occasion (doubtless when he was alone and there was but one seat to buy) he arose to the extravagance of a four-shilling box.

Consequently, despite the weightier parts of the diary, we know Pepys chiefly in his hours of ease. Sittings and consultations are so dry. If only the world would run itself decently and in silence! Even a meeting of the Committee for Tangier—when the Prince of Wales was present and such smaller fry as Chancellors—is dull and is matter for a skipping eye.

If a session of Parliament bulks to a fat paragraph and it happens that there is a bit of deviltry just below at the bottom of the page— maybe no more than a clinking of glasses (or perhaps Nell Gwynne's name pops in sight)—bless us how the eye will hurry to turn the leaf on the chance of roguery to come! Who would read through a long discourse on Admiralty business, if it be known before that Pepys is engaged with the pretty Mrs. Knipp for a trip to Bartholomew Fair to view the dancing horse, and that the start is to be made on the turning of the page? Or a piece of scandal about

Lady Castlemaine, how her nose fell out of joint when Mrs. Stuart came to court—such things tease one from the sterner business.

And for these reasons, we have been inclined to underestimate the importance of Pepys' diary. Francis Jeffrey, who wrote long ago about Pepys, evidently thought that he was an idle and unprofitable fellow and that the diary was too much given to mean and petty things. But in reality the diary is an historical mine. Even when Pepys plays upon the surface, he throws out facts that can be had nowhere else. No one would venture to write of Restoration life without digging through his pages. Pepys wrote in a confused shorthand, maybe against the eye of his wife, from whom he had reason to conceal his offenses. The papers lay undeciphered until 1825, when a partial publication was made. There were additions by subsequent editors until now it appears that the Wheatley text of 1893-1899 is final. But ever since 1825, the diary has been judged to be of high importance in the understanding of the first decade of the Restoration.

If some of the weightier parts are somewhat dry, there are places in which a lighter show of personality is coincident with real historical data. Foremost are the pages where Pepys goes to the theatre.

More than Charles II was restored in 1660. Among many things of more importance than this worthless King, the theatre was restored. Since the close of Elizabethan times it had been out of business. More than thirty years before, Puritanism had snuffed out its candles and driven its fiddlers to the streets. But Puritanism, in its turn, fell with the return of the Stuarts. Pepys is a chief witness as to what kind of theatre it was that was set up in London about the year 1660. It was far different from the Elizabethan theatre. It came in from the Bankside and the fields to the north of the city and lodged itself on the better streets and squares. It no longer patterned itself on the inn-yard, but was roofed against the rain. The time had been when the theatre was cousin to the bear-pit. They were ranged together on the Bankside and they sweat and smelled like congenial neighbors. But these days are past. Let Bartholomew Fair be as rowdy as it pleases, let acrobats and such loose fellows keep to Southwark, the theatre has risen in the world! It has put on a wig, as it were, it has tied a ribbon to itself and has become fashionable.

And although it has taken on a few extra dissolute habits, they are of the genteelest kind and will make it feel at home in the upper circles.

But also the theatre introduced movable scenery. There is an attempt toward elaboration of stage effect. "To the King's playhouse—" says Pepys, "a good scene of a town on fire." Women take parts. An avalanche of new plays descends on it. Even the old plays that have survived are garbled to suit a change of taste.

But if you would really know what kind of theatre it was that sprang up with the Stuarts and what the audiences looked like and how they behaved, you must read Pepys. With but a moderate use of fancy, you can set out with him in his yellow coach for the King's house in Drury Lane. Perhaps hunger nips you at the start. If so, you stop, as Pepys pleasantly puts it, for a "barrel of oysters." Then, having dusted yourself of crumbs, you take the road again. Presently you come to Drury Lane. Other yellow coaches are before you. There is a show of foppery on the curb and an odor of smoking links. A powdered beauty minces to the door. Once past the doorkeeper, you hear the cries of the orange women going up and down the aisles. There is a shuffling of apprentices in the gallery. A dandy who lolls in a box with a silken leg across the rail, scrawls a message to an actress and sends it off by Orange Moll. Presently Castlemaine enters the royal box with the King. There is a craning of necks, for with her the King openly "do discover a great deal of familiarity." In other boxes are other fine ladies wearing vizards to hold their modesty if the comedy is free. A board breaks in the ceiling of the gallery and dust falls in the men's hair and the ladies' necks, which, writes Pepys, "made good sport." Or again, "A gentleman of good habit, sitting just before us, eating of some fruit in the midst of the play, did drop down as dead; being choked, but with much ado Orange Moll did thrust her finger down his throat and brought him to life again." Or perhaps, "I sitting behind in a dark place, a lady spit backward upon me by a mistake, not seeing me, but after seeing her to be a very pretty lady, I was not troubled at it at all."

At a change of scenes, Mrs. Knipp spies Pepys and comes to the pit door. He goes with her to the tiring-room. "To the women's shift," he writes, "where Nell was dressing herself, and was all unready, and is very pretty, prettier than I thought…. But to see how Nell cursed for having so few people in the pit, was pretty."—"But Lord! their confidence! and how many men do hover about them as soon as they come off the stage, and how confident they are in their talk!" Or he is whispered a bit of gossip, how Castlemaine is much in love with Hart, an actor of the house. Then Pepys goes back into the pit and lays out a sixpence for an orange. As the play nears its end, footmen crowd forward at the doors. The epilogue is spoken. The fiddles squeak their last. There is a bawling outside for coaches.

"Would it fit your humor," asks Mr. Pepys, when we have been handed to our seats, "would it fit your humor, if we go around to the Rose Tavern for some burnt wine and a breast of mutton off the spit? It's sure that some brave company will fall in, and we can have a tune. We'll not heed the bellman. We'll sit late, for it will be a fine light moonshine morning."

To an Unknown Reader

Once in a while I dream that I come upon a person who is reading a book that I have written. In my pleasant dreams these persons do not nod sleepily upon my pages, and sometimes I fall in talk with them. Although they do not know who I am, they praise the book and name me warmly among my betters. In such circumstance my happy nightmare mounts until I ride foremost with the giants. If I could think that this disturbance of my sleep came from my diet and that these agreeable persons arose from a lobster or a pie, nightly at supper I would ply my fork recklessly among the platters.

But in a waking state these meetings never come. If an article of mine is ever read at all, it is read in secret like the Bible. Once, indeed, in a friend's house I saw my book upon the table, but I suspect that it had been dusted and laid out for my coming. I request my hostess that next time, for my vanity, she lay the book face down upon a chair, as though the grocer's knock intruded. Or perhaps a huckster's cart broke upon her enjoyment. Let it be thought that a rare bargain—tender asparagus or the first strawberries of the summer—tempted her off my pages! Or maybe there was red rhubarb in the cart and the jolly farmer, as he journeyed up the street, pitched it to a pleasing melody. Dear lady, I forgive you. But let us hope no laundryman led you off! Such discord would have marred my book.

I saw once in a public library, as I went along the shelves, a volume of mine which gave evidence to have been really read. The record in front showed that it had been withdrawn one time only. The card was blank below—but once certainly it had been read. I hope that the book went out on a Saturday noon when the spirits rise for the holiday to come, and that a rainy Sunday followed, so that my single reader was kept before his fire. A dull patter on the window—if one sits unbuttoned on the hearth—gives a zest to a languid chapter. The rattle of a storm—if only the room be snug—fixes the attention fast. Therefore, let the rain descend as though the heavens rehearsed for a flood! Let a tempest come out of the west! Let the chimney roar as it were a lion! And if there must be a clearing, let it hold off until the late afternoon, lest it sow too early a distaste for indoors and reading! There is scarcely a bookworm who will not slip his glasses off his nose, if the clouds break at the hour of sunset when the earth and sky are filled with a green and golden light. I took the book off the library shelf and timidly glancing across my shoulder for fear that some one might catch me, I looked along the pages. There was a thumb mark in a margin, and presently appeared a kindly stickiness on the paper as though an orange had squirted on it. Surely there had been a human being hereabouts. It was as certain as when Crusoe found the footprints in the sand. Ah, I thought, this fellow who sits in the firelight has caught an appetite. Perhaps he bit a hole and sucked the fruit, and the skin has burst behind. Or I wave the theory and now conceive that the volume was read at breakfast. If so, it is my comfort that in those dim hours it stood propped against his coffee cup.

But the trail ended with the turning of the page. There were, indeed, further on, pencil checks against one of the paragraphs as if here the book had raised a faint excitement, but I could not tell whether they sprang up in derision or in approval. Toward the end there were uncut leaves, as though even my single reader had failed in his persistence.

Being swept once beyond a usual caution, I lamented to my friend F— — of the neglect in which readers held me, to which the above experience in a library was a rare exception. F— — offered me such consolation as he could, deplored the general taste and the decadence of the times, and said that as praise was sweet to everyone, he, as far as he himself was able, offered it anonymously to those who merited it. He was standing recently in a picture gallery, when a long-haired man who stood before one of the pictures was pointed out to him as the artist who had painted it. At once F— — saw his opportunity to confer a pleasure, but as there is a touch of humor in him, he first played off a jest. Lounging forward, he dropped his head to one side as artistic folk do when they look at color. He made a knot-hole of his fingers and squinted through. Next he retreated across the room and stood with his legs apart in the very attitude of wisdom. He cast a stern eye upon the picture and gravely tapped his chin. At last when the artist was fretted to an extremity, F— — came forward and so cordially praised the picture that the artist, being now warmed and comforted, presently excused himself in a high excitement and rushed away to start another picture while the pleasant spell was on him.

Had I been the artist, I would have run from either F— —'s praise or disapproval. As an instance, I saw a friend on a late occasion coming from a bookstore with a volume of suspicious color beneath his arm. I had been avoiding that particular bookstore for a week because my book lay for sale on a forward table. And now when my friend appeared, a sudden panic seized me and I plunged into the first doorway to escape. I found myself facing a soda fountain. For a moment, in my blur, I could not account for the soda fountain, or know quite how it had come into my life. Presently an interne—for he was jacketted as if he walked a hospital—asked me what I'd have.

Still somewhat dazed, in my discomposure, having no answer ready, my startled fancy ran among the signs and labels of the counter until I recalled that a bearded man once, unblushing in my presence, had ordered a banana flip. I got the fellow's ear and named it softly. Whereupon he placed a dead-looking banana across a mound of ice-cream, poured on colored juices as though to mark the fatal wound and offered it to me. I ate a few bites of the sickish mixture until the streets were safe.

I do not know to what I can attribute my timidity. Possibly it arises from the fact that until recently my writing met with uniform rejection and failure. For years I wrote secretly in order that few persons might know how miserably I failed. I answered upon a question that I had given up the practice, that I now had no time for it, that I scribbled now and then but always burned it. All that while I gave my rare leisure and my stolen afternoons—the hours that other men give to golf and sleep and sitting together—these hours I gave to writing. On a holiday I was at it early. On Saturday when other folks were abroad, I sat at my desk. It was my grief that I was so poor a borrower of the night that I blinked stupidly on my papers if I sat beyond the usual hour. Writing was my obsession. I need no pity for my failures, for although I tossed my cap upon a rare acceptance, my deeper joy was in the writing. That joy repeated failures could not blunt.

There are paragraphs that now lie yellow in my desk with their former meaning faded, that still recall as I think of them the first exaltation when I wrote them—feverishly in a hot emotion. In those days I thought that I had caught the sunlight on my pen, and the wind and the moon and the spinning earth. I thought that the valleys and the mountains arose from the mist obedient to me. If I splashed my pen, in my warm regard it was the roar and fury of the sea. It was really no more than my youth crying out. And, alas, my thoughts and my feelings escaped me when I tried to put them down on paper, although I did not know it then. Perhaps they were too vagrant to be held. And yet these paragraphs that might be mournful records of failure, fill me with no more than a tender recollection for the boy who wrote them. The worn phrases now beg their way with broken steps. Like shrill and piping minstrels they whine and crack a melody that I still remember in its freshness.

But perhaps, reader, we are brothers in these regards. Perhaps you, too, have faded papers. Or possibly, even on a recent date, you sighed your soul into an essay or a sonnet, and you now have man-

uscript which you would like to sell. Do not mistake me! I am not
an editor, nor am I an agent for these wares. Rather I speak as a
friend who, having many such hidden sorrows, offers you a word
of comfort. To a desponding Hamlet I exclaim, "'Tis common, my
Lord." I have so many friends that have had an unproductive fling
toward letters, that I think the malady is general. So many books are
published and flourish a little while in their bright wrappers, but
yours and theirs and mine waste away in a single precious copy.

I am convinced that a close inspection of all desks—a federal matter as though Capital were under fire—would betray thousands of
abandoned novels. There may be a few stern desks that are so clut-
tered with price-sheets and stock-lists that they cannot offer harbor-
age to a love tale. Standing desks in particular, such as bookkeepers
affect, are not always chinked with these softer plots. And rarely
there is a desk so smothered in learning—reeking so of scholarship—as not to admit a lighter nook for the tucking of a sea yarn.
Even so, it was whispered to me lately that Professor B— —, whose
word shakes the continent, holds in a lower drawer no fewer than
three unpublished historical novels, each set up with a full quota of
smugglers and red bandits. One of these stories deals scandalously
with the abduction of an heiress, but this must be held in confidence. The professor is a stoic before his class, but there's blood in
the fellow.

There is, therefore, little use in your own denial. You will recall
that once, when taken to a ruined castle, you brooded on the dun-
geons until a plot popped into your head. You crammed it with
quaint phrasing from the chroniclers. You stuffed it with soldiers'
oaths. "What ho! landlord," you wrote gayly at midnight, "a foam-
ing cup, good sir. God pity the poor sailors that take the sea this
night!" And on you pelted with your plot to such conflicts and hair-
breadth escapes as lay in your contrivance.

These things you have committed. Good sir, we are of a common
piece. Let us salute as brothers! And therefore, as to a comrade, I bid
you continue in your ways. And that you may not lack matter for
your pen, I warmly urge you, when by shrewdest computation you
have exhausted the plots of adventure and have worn your villains
thin, that you proceed in quieter vein. I urge you to an April mood,

for the winds of Spring are up and daffodils nod across the garden. There is black earth in the Spring and green hilltops, and there is also the breath of flowers along the fences and the sound of water for your pen to prattle of.

A Plague of All Cowards

Having written lately against the dog, several acquaintances have asked me to turn upon the cat, and they have been good enough to furnish me with instances of her faithlessness. Also, a lady with whom I recently sat at dinner, inquired of me on the passing of the fish, whether I had ever properly considered the cow, which she esteemed a most mischievous animal. One of them had mooed at her as she crossed a pasture and she had hastily climbed a fence. I get a good many suggestions first and last. I was once taken to a Turkish bath for no other reason—as I was afterwards told—than that it might supply me with a topic. Odd books have been put in my way. A basket of school readers was once lodged with me, with a request that I direct my attention to the absurd selection of the poems. I have been urged to go against car conductors and customs men. On one occasion I received a paper of tombstone inscriptions, with a note of direction how others might be found in a neighboring churchyard if I were curious. A lady in whose company I camped last summer has asked me to give a chapter to it. We were abroad upon a lake in the full moon—we were lost upon a mountain—twice a canoe upset—there were the usual jests about cooking. These things might have filled a few pages agreeably, yet so far they have given me only a paragraph.

But I am not disposed toward any of these subjects, least of all the cat, upon which I look—despite the coldness of her nature—as a harmless and comforting appendage of the hearth-rug. I would no more prey upon her morals than I would the morals of the andirons. I choose, rather, to slip to another angle of the question and say a few words about cowards, among whom I have already confessed that I number myself.

In this year of battles, when physical courage sits so high, the reader—if he is swept off in the general opinion—will expect under such a title something caustic. He will think that I am about to loose against all cowards a plague of frogs and locusts as if old Egypt had come again. But cowardice is its own punishment. It needs no frog to nip it. Even the sharp-toothed locust—for in the days that bordered so close upon the mastodon, the locust could hardly have fallen to the tender greenling we know today—even the locust that once spoiled the Egyptians could not now add to the grief of a coward.

And yet—really I hesitate. I blush. My attack will be too intimate; for I have confessed that I am not the very button on the cap of bravery. I have indeed stiffened myself to ride a horse, a mightier feat than driving him because of the tallness of the monster and his uneasy movement, as though his legs were not well socketed and might fall out on a change of gaits. I have ridden on a camel in a side-show, but have found my only comfort in his hump. I have stroked the elephant. In a solemn hour of night I have gone downstairs to face a burglar. But I do not run singing to these dangers. While your really brave fellow is climbing a dizzy staircase to the moon—I write in figure—I would shake with fear upon a lower platform.

Perhaps you recall Mr. Tipp of the Elia essays. "Tipp," says his pleasant biographer, "never mounted the box of a stage-coach in his life; or leaned against the rails of a balcony; or walked upon the ridge of a parapet; or looked down a precipice; or let off a gun." I cannot follow Tipp, it may be, to his extreme tremors—my hair will not rise to so close a likeness of the fretful porcupine—yet in a measure we are in agreement. We are, as it were, cousins, with the mark of our common family strong on both of us.

There are persons who, when in your company on a country walk, will steal apples, not with a decent caution from a tree along the fence, but far afield. If there are grapes, they will not wait for a turn of the road, but will pluck them in the open. Or maybe in your wandering you come on a half-built house. You climb in through a window to look about. Here the stairs will go. The ice-box will be set against this wall. But if your companion is one of valor's minions, he will not be satisfied with this safe and agreeable research—this mild speculation on bath-rooms—this innocent placing of a stove. He must go aloft. He has seen a ladder and yearns to climb it. The footing on the second story is bad enough. If you fall between the joists, you will clatter to the basement. It is hard to realize that such an open breezy place will ever be cosy and warm with fires, and that sleepy folk will here lie snugly a-bed on frosty mornings. But still the brazen fellow is not content. A ladder leads horribly to the roof. For myself I will climb until the tip of my nose juts out upon the world—until it sprouts forth to the air from the topmost timbers: But I will go no farther. But if your companion sees a scaffold around a chimney, he must perch on it. For him, a dizzy plank is a pleasant belvedere from which to view the world.

The bravery of this kind of person is not confined to these few matters. If you happen to go driving with him, he will—if the horse is of the kind that distends his nostrils—on a sudden toss you the reins and leave you to guard him while he dispatches an errand. If it were a motor car there would be a brake to hold it. If it were a boat, you might throw out an anchor. A butcher's cart would have a metal drag. But here you sit defenseless—tied to the whim of a horse—greased for a runaway. The beast Dobbin turns his head and holds you with his hard eye. There is a convulsive movement along his back, a preface, it may be, to a sudden seizure. A real friend would have loosed the straps that run along the horse's flanks. Then, if any deviltry take him, he might go off alone and have it out.

I have in mind a livery stable in Kalamazoo. Myself and another man of equal equestrianism were sent once to bring out a thing called a surrey and a pair of horses. Do you happen to be acquainted with Blat's Horse Food? If your way lies among the smaller towns, you must know its merits. They are proclaimed along the fences and up the telegraph poles. Drinking-troughs speak its virtues. Horses thrive on Blat's Food. They neigh for it. A flashing lithograph is set by way of testament wherever traffic turns or lingers. Do you not recall the picture? A great red horse rears himself on his hind legs. His forward hoofs are extended. He is about to trample someone under foot. His nostrils are wide. He is unduly excited. It cannot be food, it must be drink that stirs him. He is a fearful spectacle.

There was such a picture on the wall of the stable.

"Have you any horses," I asked nervously, jerking my thumb toward the wall, "any horses that have been fed on just ordinary food? Some that are a little tired?"

For I remembered how Mr. Winkle once engaged horses to take the Pickwickians out to Manor Farm and what mishaps befell them on the way.

"'He don't shy, does he?' inquired Mr. Pickwick.

"'Shy, sir? — He wouldn't shy if he was to meet a vagginload of monkeys with their tails burnt off.'"

But how Mr. Pickwick dropped his whip, how Mr. Winkle got off his tall horse to pick it up, how he tried in vain to remount while his horse went round and round, how they were all spilt out upon the bridge and how finally they walked to Manor Farm — these things are known to everybody with an inch of reading.

"'How far is it to Dingley Dell?' they asked.

"'Better er seven mile.'

"'Is it a good road?'

"'No, t'ant.'…

"The depressed Pickwickians turned moodily away, with the tall quadruped, for which they all felt the most unmitigated disgust, following slowly at their heels."

"Have you any horses," I repeated, "that have not been fed on Blat's Food — horses that are, so to speak, on a diet?"

In the farthest stalls, hidden from the sunlight and the invigorating infection of the day, two beasts were found with sunken chests and hollow eyes, who took us safely to our destination on their hands and knees.

As you may suspect, I do not enjoy riding. There is, it is true, one saddle horse in North Carolina that fears me. If time still spares him, that horse I could ride with content. But I would rather trust myself on the top of a wobbly step-ladder than up the sides of most horses. I am not quite of a mind, however, with Samuel Richardson who owned a hobby-horse and rode on his hearth-rug in the intervals of writing "Pamela." It is likely that when he had rescued her from an adventure of more than usual danger—perhaps her villainous master has been concealed in her closet—perhaps he has been hiding beneath her bed—it is likely, having brought her safely off, the author locked her in the buttery against a fresh attack. Then he felt, good man, in need of exercise. So while he waits for tea and muffins, he leaps upon his rocking-horse and prances off. As for the hobby-horse itself, I have not heard whether it was of the usual nursery type, or whether it was built in the likeness of the leather camels of a German steamship.

I need hardly say that these confessions of my cowardice are for your ear alone. They must not get abroad to smirch me. If on a country walk I have taken to my heels, you must not twit me with poltroonery. If you charge me with such faint-heartedness while other persons are present, I'll deny it flat. When I sit in the company of ladies at dinner, I dissemble my true nature, as doublet and hose ought to show itself courageous to petticoat. If then, you taunt me, for want of a better escape, I shall turn it to a jest. I shall engage the table flippantly: Hear how preposterously the fellow talks!—he jests to satisfy a grudge. In appearance I am whole as the marble, founded as a rock.

But really some of us cowards are diverting persons. The lady who directed me against the cow is a most delightful woman with whom I hope I shall again sit at dinner. A witty lady of my acquaintance shivers when a cat walks in the room. A man with whom I pass the time pleasantly and profitably, although he will not admit a fear of ghosts, still will not sleep in an empty house because of possible noises. I would rather spend a Saturday evening in the company of the cowardly Falstaff than of the bold Hotspur. If it were not for sack, villainous sack, and a few spots upon his front, you would go far to find a better companion than the fat old Knight. Bob Acres was not much for valor and he made an ass of himself when he went to fight a duel, yet one could have sat agreeably at mutton with him.

But these things are slight. It matters little whether or not one can mount a ladder comfortably. Now that motors have come in, horses stand remotely in our lives. Nor is it of great moment whether or not we fear to be out of fashion—whether we halt in the wearing of a wrong-shaped hat, or glance fearfully around when we choose from a line of forks. Superstitions rest mostly on the surface and are not deadly in themselves. A man can be true of heart even if he will not sit thirteen at table. But there is a kind of fear that is disastrous to them that have it. It is the fear of the material universe in all its manifestations. There are persons, stout both of chest and limb, who fear drafts and wet feet. A man who is an elephant of valor and who has been feeling this long while a gentle contempt for such as myself, will cry out if a soft breeze strikes against his neck. If a foot slips to the gutter and becomes wet, he will dose himself. Achilles did not more carefully nurse his heel. For him the lofty dome of air is packed with malignant germs. The round world is bottled with contagion. A strong man who, in his time, might have slain the Sofi, is as fearful of his health as though the plague were up the street. Calamities beset him. The slightest sniffling in his nose is the trumpet for a deep disorder. Existence is but a moving hazard. Life for him, poor fellow, is but a room with a window on the night and a storm beating on the casement. God knows, it is better to grow giddy on a ladder than to think that this majestic earth is such an universal pestilence.

The Asperities of the Early British Reviewers

Book reviewers nowadays direct their attention, for the most part, to the worthy books and they habitually neglect those that seem beneath their regard. On a rare occasion they assail an unprofitable book, but even this is often but a bit of practice. They swish a bludgeon to try their hand. They only take their

anger, as it were, upon an outing, lest with too close housing it grow pallid and shrink in girth. Or maybe they indulge themselves in humor. Perhaps they think that their pages grow dull and that ridicule will restore the balance. They throw it in like a drunken porter to relieve a solemn scene. I fancy that editors of this baser sort keep on their shelves one or two volumes for their readers' sport and mirth. I read recently a review of an historical romance — a last faltering descendant of the race — whose author in an endeavor to restore the past, had made too free a use of obsolete words. With what playfulness was he held up to scorn! Mary come up, sweet chuck! How his quaint phrasing was turned against him! What a merry fellow it is who writes, how sharp and caustic! There's pepper on his mood.

But generally, it is said, book reviews are too flattering. Professor Bliss Perry, being of this opinion, offered some time ago a statement that "Magazine writing about current books is for the most part bland, complaisant, pulpy…. The Pedagogue no longer gets a chance at the gifted young rascal who needs, first and foremost, a premonitory whipping; the youthful genius simply stays away from school and carries his unwhipped talents into the market place." At a somewhat different angle of the same opinion, Dr. Crothers suggests in an essay that instead of being directed to the best books, we need to be warned from the worst. He proposes to set up a list of the Hundred Worst Books. For is it not better, he asks, to put a lighthouse on a reef than in the channel? The open sea does not need a bell-buoy to sound its depth.

On these hints I have read some of the book criticisms of days past to learn whether they too were pulpy — whether our present silken criticism always wore its gloves and perfumed itself, or whether it has fallen to this smiling senility from a sterner youth. Although I am usually a rusty student, yet by diligence I have sought to mend my knowledge that I might lay it out before you. Lately, therefore, if you had come within our Public Library, you would have found me in one of these attempts. Here I went, scrimping the other business of the day in order that I might be at my studies before the rush set in up town. Mine was the alcove farthest from the door, where are the mustier volumes that fit a bookish student. So if your quest was the lighter books — such verse and novels as present fame attests—you did not find me. I was hooped and bowed around the corner. I am no real scholar, but I study on a spurt. For a whole week together I may read old plays until their jigging style infects my own. I have set myself against the lofty histories, although I tire upon their lower slopes and have not yet persisted to their upper and windier ridges. I have, also, a pretty knowledge of the Queen Anne wits and feel that I must have dogged and spied upon them while they were yet alive. But in general, although I am curious in the earlier chapters of learning, I lag in the inner windings. However, for a fortnight I have sat piled about with old reviews, whose leather rots and smells, in order that I might study the fading criticisms of the past.

Until rather near the end of the eighteenth century, those who made their living in England by writing were chiefly publishers' hacks, fellows of the Dunciad sucking their quills in garrets and selling their labor for a crust, for the reading public was too small to support them. Or they found a patron and gave him a sugared sonnet for a pittance, or strained themselves to the length of an Ode for a berth in his household. Or frequently they supported a political party and received a place in the Red Tape Office. But even in politics, on account of the smallness of the reading public and the politicians' indifference to its approval, their services were of slight account. Too often a political office was granted from a pocket borough in which a restricted electorate could be bought at a trifling expense. To gain support inside the House of Commons was enough. The greater public outside could be ignored. This attitude changed with the coming of the French Revolution. Here was a new force unrealized before—that of a crowd which, being unrepresented and with a real grievance, could, when it liked, take a club and go after what it wanted. For the first time in many years in England—such were the whiffs of liberty across the Channel—the power of an unrepresented public came to be known. It was not that the English crowd had as yet taken the club in its hands, but there were new thoughts abroad in the world, and there was the possibility to be regarded. To influence this larger public, therefore, men who could write came little by little into a larger demand. And as writers were comparatively scarce, all kinds—whether they wrote poems or prose—were pressed into service. It is significant, too, that it was in the decades subjected to the first influence of the French Revolution that the English daily paper took its start as an agent to influence public opinion.

It was therefore rather more than one hundred years ago that writers came to a better prosperity. They came out of their garrets, took rooms on the second floor, polished their brasses and became Persons. I can fancy that a writer after spending a morning in the composition of a political article on the whisper of a Cabinet Minister, wrote a sonnet after lunch, and a book review before dinner. Let us see in what mood they took their advancement! Let us examine their temper—but in book reviewing only, for that alone concerns us! In doing this, we have the advantage of knowing the final estimate of the books they judged. Like the witch, we have looked into the seeds of time and we know "which grain will grow and which will not."

In 1802, when the Edinburgh Review (which was the first of its line to acquire distinction) came into being, the passion of the times found voice in politics. Both Whigs and Tories had been alarmed by the excesses of the French Revolution; both feared that England was drifting the way of France; each had a remedy, but opposed and violently maintained. The Tories put the blame of the Revolution on the compromises of Louis XVI, and accordingly they were hostile to any political change. The Whigs, on the other hand, saw the rottenness of England as a cause that would incite her to revolution also, and they advocated reform while yet there was time. The general fear of a revolution gave the government of England to the Tories, and kept them in power for several decades. And England was ripe for trouble. The government was but nominally representative. No Catholic, Jew, Dissenter or poor man had a vote or could hold a seat in Parliament. Industrially and economically the country was in the condition of France in the year of Arthur Young's journey. The poverty was abject, the relief futile and the hatred of the poor for the rich was inflammatory. George III, slipping into feebleness and insanity, yet jealous of his unconstitutional power, was a vacillating despot, quarrelling with his Commons and his Ministers. Lord Eldon as Chancellor, but with as nearly the control of a Premier as the King would allow, was the staunch upholder of all things that have since been disproved and discarded. Bagehot said of him that "he believed in everything which it is impossible to believe in." France and Napoleon threatened across the narrow channel. England still growled at the loss of her American colonies. It was as yet the England of the old regime. The great reforms were to come thirty years later—the Catholic Emancipation, the abolishment of slavery in the colonies, the suppression of the pocket boroughs, the gross bribery of elections, the cleaning of the poor laws and the courts of justice.

It was in this dark hour of English history that the writers polished their brasses and set up as Persons. And if the leading articles that they wrote of mornings stung and snapped with venom, it is natural that the book reviews on which they spent their afternoons had also some vinegar in them, especially if they concerned books written by those of the opposition. And other writers, even if they had no political connection, borrowed their manners from those who had. It was the animosities of party politics that set the general tone. Billingsgate that had grown along the wharves of the lower river, was found to be of service in Parliament and gave a spice and sparkle even to a book review. Presently a large part of literary England wore the tags of political preference. Writers were often as clearly distinguished as were the ladies in the earlier day, when Addison wrote his paper on party patches. There were seats of Moral Philosophy to be handed out, under-secretaryships, consular appointments. It is not enough to say that Francis Jeffrey was a reviewer, he was as well a Whig and was running a Review that was Whig from the front cover to the back. Leigh Hunt was not merely a poet, for he was also a radical, and therefore in the opinions of Tories, a believer in immorality and indecency. No matter how innocent a title might appear, it was held in suspicion, on the chance that it assailed the Ministry or endangered the purity of England. William Gifford was more than merely the editor of the Quarterly Review, for he was as well a Tory editor whose duty it was to pry into Whiggish roguery. Lockhart and Wilson, who wrote in Blackwood's, were Tories tooth and nail, biting and scratching for party. Nowadays, literature, having found the public to be its most profitable patron, works hard and even abjectly for its favor. Although there are defects in the arrangement, it must be confessed that the divorce of literature from politics contributes to the general peace of the household.

The Edinburgh Review was founded in 1802, the Quarterly Review in 1809, Blackwood's Magazine in 1817. These three won distinction among others of less importance, and from them only I quote. In 1802, when Tory rule was strongest and Lord Eldon flourished, there was living in Edinburgh a group of young men who were for the most part briefless barristers. Their case was worse because they were Whigs. Few cases came their way and no offices. These young men were Francis Jeffrey, Francis Horner, Henry Brougham, and there was also Sydney Smith who had just come to Edinburgh from an English country parish. The eldest was thirty-one, the youngest twenty-three. Although all of them had brilliant lives before them, not one of them had made as yet more than a step toward his accomplishment. Sydney Smith had been but lately an obscure curate, buried in the middle of Salisbury Plain, away from all contact with the world. Francis Jeffrey had been a hack writer in London, had studied medicine, had sought unsuccessfully a government position in India, had written poor sonnets, and was now lounging with but a scanty occupation in the halls of the law courts. Francis Horner had just come to the Scottish bar straight from his studies. Henry Brougham, who in days to come was to be Lord Chancellor of England and to whose skill in debate the passing of the Great Reform bill of 1832 is partly due, is also just admitted to the practice of the law.

The founding of the Review was casual. These men were accustomed to meet of an evening for general discussion and speculation. It happened one night as they sat together—the place was a garret if legend is to be believed—that Sydney Smith lamented that their discussions came to nothing, for they were all Whigs, all converted to the cause; whereas if they could only bring their opinions to the outside public they could stir opinion. From so slight a root the Review sprouted. Sydney Smith was made editor and kept the position until after the appearance of the first number, when Jeffrey succeeded him. The Review became immediately a power, appearing quarterly and striking its blows anonymously against a sluggish government, lashing the Tory writers, and taking its part, which is of greater consequence, in the promulgation of the Whig reforms which were to ripen in thirty years and convert the old into modern England. In the destruction of outworn things, it was, as it were, a magazine of Whig explosives.

The Quarterly Review was the next to come and it was Tory. John Murray, the London publisher, had been the English distributor of the Edinburgh Review. In 1809, two considerations moved him to found in London a review to rival the Scotch periodical. First the Tory party was being hard hit by the Edinburgh Review and there was need of defense and retaliation. In the second place, John Murray saw that if his publishing house was to flourish, it must provide this new form of literature that had become so popular. For the very shortness of the essays and articles, in which extensive conditions were summarized for quick digestion, had met with English approval as well as Scotch. People had become accustomed, says Bagehot, of taking "their literature in morsels, as they take sandwiches on a journey." Murray appealed to George Canning, then in office, for assistance and was introduced to William Gifford as a man capable of the undertaking, who would also meet the favor of the government party. The rise of the Quarterly Review was not brilliant. It did not fill the craving for novelty, inasmuch as the Edinburgh was already in the field. Furthermore, there is not the opportunity in defense for as conspicuous gallantry as in offensive warfare.

It was eight years before another enduring review was started. William Blackwood of Edinburgh had grown like Murray from a bookseller to a publisher, and he, too, looked for a means of increasing his prestige. He had launched a review the year previously, in 1816, but it had foundered when it was scarcely off the ways. His second attempt he was determined must be successful. His new editors were John G. Lockhart and John Wilson, and the new policy, although nominally Tory, was first and last the magazine's notoriety. It hawked its wares into public notice by sensational articles and personal vilification. Wilson was thirty-two and Lockhart twenty-three, yet they were as mischievous as boys. In their pages is found the most abominable raving that has ever passed for literary criticism. They did not need any party hatred to fire them. William Blackwood welcomed any abuse that took his magazine out of "the calm of respectable mediocrity." Anything that stung or startled was welcome to a place in its pages.

So Blackwood's was published and Edinburgh city, we may be sure, set up a roar of delight and anger. Never before had one's friends been so assailed. Never before had one's enemies been so grilled. How pleasing for a Tory fireside was the mud bath with which it defiled Coleridge, who was—and you had always known it—"little better than a rogue." One's Tory dinner was the more toothsome for the hot abuse of the Chaldee Manuscript. What stout Tory, indeed, would doze of an evening on such a sheet! There followed of course cases of libel. The editors even found it safer, after the publication of the first number, to retire for a time to the country until the city cooled.

I choose now to turn to the pages of these three reviews and set out before you samples of their criticisms, in order that you may contrast them with our own literary judgments. I warn you in fairness that I have been disposed to choose the worst, yet there are hundreds of other criticisms but little better. Of the three reviews, Blackwood's was the least seriously political in its policy, yet its critical vilifications are the worst. The Edinburgh Review, the most able of the three and the most in earnest in politics, is the least vituperative. With this introduction, let us shake the pepperpot and lay out the strong vinegar of our feast!

In the judgment of the Edinburgh Review, Tom Moore, who had just published his "Odes and Epistles" but had not yet begun his Irish melodies, is a man who "with some brilliancy of fancy, and some show of classical erudition … may boast, if the boast can please him, of being the most licentious of modern versifiers, and the most poetical of those who, in our times, have devoted their talents to the propagation of immorality. We regard his book, indeed, as a public nuisance…. He sits down to ransact the impure places of his memory for inflammatory images and expressions, and commits them laboriously in writing, for the purpose of insinuating pollution into the minds of unknown and unsuspecting readers."

Francis Jeffrey wrote this, and Moore challenged him to fight. The police interfered, and as Jeffrey put it, "the affair ended amicably. We have since breakfasted together very lovingly. He has expressed penitence for what he has written and declared that he will never again apply any little talents he may possess to such purpose: and I

have said that I shall be happy to praise him whenever I find that he
has abjured these objectionable topics." It was Sydney Smith who
said of Jeffrey he would "damn the solar system—bad light—
planets too distant—pestered with comets. Feeble contrivance—
could make a better with great ease."

Jeffrey reviewed Wordsworth and found in the "Lyrical Ballads"
"vulgarity, affectation and silliness." He is alarmed, moreover, lest
his "childishness, conceit and affectation" spread to other authors.
He proposes a poem to be called "Elegiac Stanzas to a Sucking Pig,"
and of "Alice Fell" he writes that "if the publishing of such trash as
this be not felt as an insult on the public taste, we are afraid it cannot be insulted." When the "White Doe of Rylstone" was published—no prime favorite, I confess, of my own—Jeffrey wrote that it
had the merit of being the very worst poem he ever saw imprinted
in a quarto volume. "It seems to us," he wrote, "to consist of a happy
union of all the faults, without any of the beauties, which belong to
his school of poetry. It is just such a work, in short, as some wicked
enemy of that, school might be supposed to have devised, on purpose to make it ridiculous."

Lord Byron, on the publication of an early volume, is counselled
"that he do forthwith abandon poetry ... the mere rhyming of the
final syllable, even when accompanied by the presence of a certain
number of feet ... is not the whole art of poetry. We would entreat
him to believe," continued the reviewer, "that a certain portion of
liveliness, somewhat of fancy, is necessary to constitute a poem; and
that a poem in the present day, to be read, must contain at least one
thought...." It was this attack that brought forth Byron's "English
Bards and Scotch Reviewers."

As long as Jeffrey hoped to enlist Southey to write for the Edinburgh Review, he treated him with some favor. But Southey took up
with the Quarterly. "The Laureate," says the Edinburgh presently,
"has now been out of song for a long time: But we had comforted
ourselves with the supposition that he was only growing fat and
lazy.... The strain, however, of this publication, and indeed of some
that went before it, makes us apprehensive that a worse thing has
befallen him ... that the worthy inditer of epics is falling gently into
dotage."

Now for the Quarterly Review, if by chance it can show an equal spleen!

There lived in the early days of the nineteenth century a woman by the name of Lady Morgan, who was the author of several novels and books of travel. Although her record in intelligence and morals is good, John Croker, who regularly reviewed her books, accuses her works of licentiousness, profligacy, irreverence, blasphemy, libertinism, disloyalty and atheism. There are twenty-six pages of this in one review only, and any paragraph would be worth the quoting for its ferocity. After this attack it was Macaulay who said he hated Croker like "cold boiled veal."

The Quarterly reviewed Keats' "Endymion," although the writer naively states at the outset that he has not read the poem. "Not that we have been wanting in our duty," he writes, "far from it—indeed, we have made efforts almost as superhuman as the story itself appears to be, to get through it; but with the fullest stretch of our perseverance we are forced to confess that we have not been able to struggle beyond the first of the four books...." Finally he questions whether Keats is the author's name, for he doubts "that any man in his senses would put his real name to such a rhapsody."

Leigh Hunt's "Rimini" the Quarterly finds to be an "ungrammatical, unauthorized, chaotic jargon, such as we believe was never before spoken, much less written.... We never," concludes the reviewer, "in so few lines saw so many clear marks of the vulgar impatience of a low man, conscious and ashamed of his wretched vanity, and labouring, with coarse flippancy, to scramble over the bounds of birth and education, and fidget himself into the stoutheartedness of being familiar with a Lord." In a later review, Hunt is a propounder of atheism. "Henceforth," says the reviewer, "... he may slander a few more eminent characters, he may go on to deride venerable and holy institutions, he may stir up more discontent and sedition, but he will have no peace of mind within ... he will live and die unhonoured in his own generation, and, for his own sake it is to be hoped, moulder unknown in those which are to follow."

Hazlitt belongs to a "class of men by whom literature is more than at any period disgraced." His style is suited for washerwomen, a "class of females with whom ... he and his friend Mr. Hunt particularly delight to associate."

Shelley, writes the Quarterly, "is one of that industrious knot of authors, the tendency of whose works we have in our late Numbers exposed to the caution of our readers ... for with perfect deliberation and the steadiest perseverance he perverts all the gifts of his nature, and does all the injury, both public and private, which his faculties enable him to perpetrate." His "poetry is in general a mere jumble of words and heterogeneous ideas." "The Cloud" is "simple nonsense." "Prometheus Unbound" is a "great storehouse of the obscure and unintelligible." In the "Sensitive Plant" there is "no meaning." And for Shelley himself, he is guilty of a great many terrible things, including verbiage, impiety, immorality and absurdity.

Of Blackwood's Magazine the special victims were Keats and Hunt and Coleridge. "Mr. Coleridge," says the reviewer, "... seems to believe that every tongue is wagging in his praise — that every ear is open to imbibe the oracular breathings of his inspiration ... no sound is so sweet to him as that of his own voice ... he seems to consider the mighty universe itself as nothing better than a mirror in which, with a grinning and idiot self-complacency, he may contemplate the physiognomy of Samuel Taylor Coleridge.... Yet insignificant as he assuredly is, he cannot put pen to paper without a feeling that millions of eyes are fixed upon him...."

Leigh Hunt, says Blackwood, "is a man of extravagant pretensions ... exquisitely bad taste and extremely vulgar modes of thinking." His "Rimini" "is so wretchedly written that one feels disgust at its pretense, affectation and gaudiness, ignorance, vulgarity, irreverence, quackery, glittering and rancid obscenities."

Blackwood's wrote of the "calm, settled, imperturbable, drivelling idiocy of Endymion," and elsewhere of Keats' "prurient and vulgar lines, evidently meant for some young lady east of Temple Bar.... It is a better and a wiser thing," it commented, "to be a starved apothecary than a starved poet; so back to the shop, Mr. John, back to 'plasters, pills and ointment boxes.'" And even when Shelley wrote his "Adonais" on the death of Keats, Blackwood's met it with a contemptible parody:

"Weep for my Tom cat! all ye Tabbies weep!"

Perhaps I have quoted enough. This is the parentage of our silken and flattering criticism.

The pages of these old reviews rest yellow on the shelves. From them there comes a smell of rotting leather, as though the infection spreads. The hour grows late. Like the ghost of the elder Hamlet, I detect the morning to be near.

The Pursuit of Fire

Reader, if by chance you have the habit of writing — whether they be sermons to hurl across your pews, or sonnets in the Spring — doubtless you have moments when you sit at your desk bare of thoughts. Mother Hubbard's cupboard when she went to seek the bone was not more empty. In such plight you chew your pencil as though it were stuff to feed your brain. Or if you are of delicate taste, you fall upon your fingers. Or in the hope that exercise will stir your wits, you pace up and down the room and press your nose upon the window if perhaps the grocer's boy shall rouse you. Some persons draw pictures on their pads or put pot-hooks on their letters — for talent varies — or they roughen up their hair. I knew one gifted fellow whose shoes presently would cramp him until he kicked them off, when at once the juices of his intellect would flow. Genius, I am told, sometimes locks its door and, if unrestrained, peels its outer wrappings. Or, in your poverty, you run through the pages of a favorite volume, with a notebook for a sly theft to start you off. In what dejection you have fallen! It is best that you put on your hat and take your stupid self abroad.

Or maybe you think that your creative fire will blaze, if instead of throwing in your wet raw thoughts, you feed it a few seasoned bits. You open, therefore, the drawer of your desk where you keep your rejected and broken fragments — for your past has not been prosperous — hopeful against experience that you can recast one of these to your present mood. This is mournful business. Certain paragraphs that came from you hot are now patched and shivery. Their finer meaning has run out between the lines as though these spaces were sluices for the proper drainage of the page. You had best put on your hat. You will get no comfort from these stale papers.

One evening lately, being in this plight, I spread out before me certain odds and ends. I had dug deeper than usual in the drawer and had brought up a yellow stratum of a considerable age. I was poring upon these papers and was wondering whether I could fit them to a newer measure, when I heard a slight noise behind me. I glanced around and saw that a man had entered the room and was now seated in a chair before the fire. In the common nature of things this should have been startling, for the hour was late — twelve o'clock had struck across the way — and I had thought that I was quite alone. But there was something so friendly and easy in his attitude — he was a young man, little more than a lanky boy — that instead of being frightened, I swung calmly around for a better look. He sat with his legs stretched before him and with his chin resting in his hand, as though in thought. By the light that fell on him from the fire, I saw that he wore a brown checked suit and that he was clean and respectable in appearance. His face was in shadow.

"Good evening," I said, "you startled me."

"I am sorry," he replied. "I beg your pardon. I was going by and I saw your light. I wished to make your acquaintance. But I saw at once that I was intruding, so I sat here. You were quite absorbed. Would you mind if I mended the fire?"

Without waiting for an answer, he took the poker and dealt the logs several blows. It didn't greatly help the flame, but he poked with such enjoyment that I smiled. I have myself rather a liking for stirring a fire. He set another log in place. Then he drew from his pocket a handful of dried orange peel. "I love to see it burn," he said. "It crackles and spits." He ranged the peel upon the log where the flame would get it, and then settled himself in the big chair.

"Perhaps you smoke?" I asked, pushing toward him a box of cigarettes.

He smiled. "I thought that you would know my habits. I don't smoke."

"So you were going by and came up to see me?" I asked.

"Yes. I was not sure that I would know you. You are a little older than I thought, a little—stouter, but dear me, how you have lost your hair! But you have quite forgotten me."

"My dear boy," I said, "you have the advantage of me. Where have I seen you? There is something familiar about you and I am sure that I have seen that brown suit before."

"We have never really known each other," the boy replied. "We met once, but only for an instant. But I have thought of you since that meeting a great many times. I lay this afternoon on a hilltop and wondered what you would be like. But I hoped that sometimes you would think of me. Perhaps you have forgotten that I used to collect railway maps and time-tables."

"Did you?" I replied. "So did I when I was a little younger than you are.
Perhaps if I might see your face, I would know you."

"It's nothing for show," he replied, and he kept it still in shadow. "Would you mind," he said at length, "if I ate an apple?" He took one from his pocket and broke it in his hands. "You eat half," he said.

I accepted the part he offered me. "Perhaps you would like a knife and plate," I said. "I can find them in the pantry."

"Not for me," he replied. "I prefer to eat mine this way." He took an enveloping bite.

"I myself care nothing for plates," I said. We ate in silence. Presently: "You have my habit," I said, "of eating everything, skin, seeds and all."

"Everything but the stem," he replied.

By this time the orange peel was hissing and exploding.

"You are an odd boy," I said. "I used to put orange peel away to dry in order to burn it. We seem to be as like as two peas."

"I wonder," he said, "if that is so." He turned in his chair and faced me, although his face was still in shadow. "Doubtless, we are far different in many things. Do you swallow grape seeds?"

"Hardly!" I cried. "I spit them out."

"I am glad of that." He paused. "It was a breezy hilltop where I lay. I thought of you all afternoon. You are famous, of course?"

"Dear me, no!"

"Oh, I'm so sorry. I had hoped you might be. I had counted on it. It is very disappointing. I was thinking about that as I lay on the hill. But aren't you just on the point of doing something that will make you famous?"

"By no means."

"Dear me, I am so sorry. Do you happen to be married?"

"Yes."

"And would you mind telling me her name?"

I obliged him.

"I don't remember to have heard of her. I didn't think of that name once as I lay upon the hill. Things don't turn out as one might expect. Now, I would have thought—but it's no matter."

For a moment or so he was lost in thought, and then he spoke again: "You were writing when I came into the room?"

"Nothing important."

The boy ran his fingers in his hair and threw out his arms impatiently. "That's what I would like to do. I am in college, and I try for one of the papers. But my stuff comes back. But this summer in the vacation, I am working in an office. I run errands and when there is nothing else to do, I study a big invoice book, so as to get the names of things that are bought. There is a racket of drays and wagons outside the windows, and along in the middle of the afternoon I get tired and thick in my head. But I write Saturday afternoons and Sunday mornings."

The boy stopped and fixed his eyes on me. "I don't suppose that you happen to be a poet?"

"Not at all," I replied. "But perhaps you are one. Tell me about it!"

The boy took a turn at the fire with the poker, but it was chiefly in embarrassment. Presently he returned to his chair. He stretched his long arms upward above his head.

"No, I'm not," he said. "And yet sometimes I think that I have a kind of poetry in me. Only I can't get it into words. I lay thinking about that, too, on the hillside. There was a wind above my head, and I thought that I could almost put words to the tune. But I have never written a single poem. Yet, goodness me, what thoughts I have! But they aren't real thoughts—what you would regularly call thoughts. Things go racing and tingling in my head, but I can never get them down. They are just feelings."

As he spoke, the boy gazed intently through the chimney bricks out into another world. The fireplace was its portal and he seemed to wait for the fires to cool before entering into its possession. It was several moments before he spoke again.

"I don't want you to think me ridiculous, but so few understand. If only I could master the tools! Perhaps my thoughts are old, but they come to me with such freshness and they are so unexpected. Could I only solve the frets and spaces inside me here, I could play what tune I chose. But my feelings are cold and stale before I can get them into thoughts. I have no doubt, however, that they are just as real as those other feelings that in time, after much scratching, get into final form and become poetry. I know of course that a man's reach should exceed his grasp—it's hackneyed enough—but just for once I would like to pull down something when I have been up on tiptoe for a while.

"Sometimes I get an impression of pity—a glance up a dark hallway—an old woman with a shawl upon her head—a white face at a window—a blind fiddler in the street—but the impression is gone in a moment. Or a touch of beauty gets me. It may be nothing but a street organ in the spring. Perhaps you like street organs, too?"

"I do, indeed!" I cried. "There was one today outside my window and my feet kept wiggling to it."

The boy clapped his hands. "I knew that you would be like that. I hoped for it on the hill. As for me, when I hear one, I'm so glad that

I could cry out. In its lilt there is the rhythm of life. It moves me more than a hillside with its earliest flowers. Am I absurd? It is equal to the pipe of birds, to shallow waters and the sound of wind to stir me to thoughts of April. Today as I came downtown, I saw several merry fellows dancing on the curb. There are tunes, too, upon the piano that send me off. I play a little myself. I see you have a piano. Do you still play?"

"A little, rather sadly," I replied.

"That's too bad, but perhaps you sing?"

"Even worse."

"Dear me, that's too bad. I have rather a voice myself. Well, as I was saying, when I hear those tunes, I curl up with the smoke and blow forth from the chimney. If I walk upon the street when the wind is up, and see a light fleece of smoke coming from a chimney top, I think that down below someone is listening to music that he likes, and that his thoughts ride upon the night, like those white streamers of smoke. And then I think of castles and mountains and high places and the sounds of storm. Or in fancy I see a tower that tapers to the moon with a silver gleam upon it."

The strange boy lay back and laughed. "Musicians think that they are the only ones that can hear the finer sounds. If one of us common fellows cocks his ear, they think that only the coarser thumps get inside. And artists think that they alone know the glory of color. I was thinking of that, this afternoon. And yet I have walked under the blue sky. I have seen twilights that these men of paint would botch on canvas. But both musicians and artists have a vision that is greater than their product. The soul of a man can hardly be recorded in black and white keys. Nor can a little pigment which you rub upon your thumb be the measure of an artist. So I suppose that is the way also with poets. It is not to be expected that they can express themselves fully in words that they have borrowed from the kitchen. When their genius flames up, it is only the lesser sparks that fall upon their writing pads. It consoles me that a man should be greater than his achievement. I who have done so little would otherwise be so forlorn."

"It's odd," I said, when he had fallen into silence, "that I used to feel exactly as you do. It stirs an old recollection. If I am not mistaken, I once wrote a paper on the subject."

The boy smiled dreamily. "But if small persons like myself," he began, "can have such frenzies, how must it be with those greater persons who have amazed the world? I have wondered in what kind of exaltation Shakespeare wrote his storm in 'Lear.' There must have been a first conception greater even than his accomplishment. Did he look from his windows at a winter tempest and see miserable old men and women running hard for shelter? Did a flash of lightning bare his soul to the misery, the betrayal and the madness of the world? His supreme moment was not when he flung the completed manuscript aside, or when he heard the actors mouth his lines, but in the flash and throb of creation—in the moment when he knew that he had the power in him to write 'Lear.' What we read is the cold forging, wonderful and enduring, but not to be compared to the producing furnace."

The boy had spoken so fast that he was out of breath.

"Hold a bit!" I cried. "What you have said sounds familiar. Where could I have heard it before?"

There was something almost like a sneer on the boy's face. "What a memory you have! And perhaps you recall this brown suit, too. It's ugly enough to be remembered. Now please let me finish what came to me this afternoon on the hill! Prometheus," he continued, "scaled the heavens and brought back fire to mortals. And he, as the story goes, clutched at a lightning bolt and caught but a spark. And even that, glorious. Mankind properly accredits him with a marvellous achievement. It is for this reason that I comfort myself although I have not yet written a single line of verse."

"My dear fellow," I said, "please tell me where I have read something like what you have spoken?"

The boy's answer was irrelevant. "You first tell me what you did with a brown checked suit you once owned."

"I never owned but one brown suit," I replied, "and that was when I was still in college. I think that I gave it away before it was worn out."

The boy once more clapped his hands. "Oh, I knew it, I knew it. I'll give mine tomorrow to the man who takes our ashes. Now, won't you please play the piano for me?"

"Assuredly. Choose your tune!"

He fumbled a bit in the rack and passing some rather good music, he held up a torn and yellow sheet. "This is what I want," he said.

I had not played it for many years. After a false start or so—for it was villainously set in four sharps for which I have an aversion—I got through it. On a second trial I did better.

The boy made no comment. He had sunk down in his chair until he was quite out of sight. "Well," I said, "what next?"

There was no answer.

I arose from the bench and glanced in his direction. "Hello," I cried, "what has become of you?"

The chair was empty. I turned on all the lights. He was nowhere in sight. I shook the hangings. I looked under my desk, for perhaps the lad was hiding from me in jest. It was unlikely that he could have passed me to gain the door, but I listened at the sill for any sound upon the stairs. The hall was silent. I called without response. Somewhat bewildered I came back to the hearth. Only a few minutes before, as it seemed, there had been a brisk fire with a row of orange peel upon the upper log. Now all trace of the peel was gone and the logs had fallen to a white ash.

I was standing perplexed, when I observed that a little pile of papers lay on the rug just off the end of my desk as by a careless elbow. At least, I thought, this impolite fellow has forgotten some of his possessions. It will serve him right if it is poetry that he wrote upon the hilltop.

I picked up the papers. They were yellow and soiled, and writing was scrawled upon them. At the top was a date—but it was twenty years old. I turned to the last sheet. At least I could learn the boy's name. To my amazement, I saw at the bottom in an old but familiar writing, not the boy's name, but my own.

I gazed at the chimney bricks and their substance seemed to part before my eyes. I looked into a world beyond—a fabric of moonlight and hilltop and the hot fret of youth. Perhaps the boy had only been waiting for the fire upon the hearth to cool to enter this other world of his restless ambition and desire.

Reader, if by chance you have the habit of writing—let us confine ourselves now to sonnets and such airy matter as rides upon the night—doubtless, you sit sometimes at your desk bare of thoughts. The juices of your intellect are parched and dry. In such plight, I beg you not to fall upon your fingers or to draw pictures on your sheet. But most vehemently, and with such emphasis as I possess, I beg you not to rummage among your rejected and broken fragments in the hope of recasting a withered thought to a present mood. Rather, before you sour and curdle, it is good to put on your hat and take your stupid self abroad.